SELBY'S SHEMOZZLE

DUNCAN BALL

with illustrations by Allan Stomann

Angus&Robertson
An imprint of HarperCollins*Publishers*

Angus&Robertson
An imprint of HarperCollins*Publishers*, Australia

First published in Australia in 2005
by HarperCollins*Publishers* Pty Limited
ABN 36 009 913 517
A member of the HarperCollins*Publishers* (Australia) Pty Limited Group
www.harpercollins.com.au

HarperCollins*Publishers*
25 Ryde Road, Pymble, Sydney, NSW 2073, Australia
31 View Road, Glenfield, Auckland 10, New Zealand
77–85 Fulham Palace Road, London W6 8JB, United Kingdom
2 Bloor Street East, 20th floor, Toronto, Ontario M4W 1A8, Canada
10 East 53rd Street, New York NY 10022, USA

National Library of Australia Cataloguing-in-Publication data:

Ball, Duncan, 1941– .
   Selby's shemozzle.
   ISBN 0 2072 0030 0.
   1. Dogs – Juvenile fiction. I. Stomann, Allan. II. Title.
A823.3

Cover design by Christa Moffitt, Christabella Designs
Cover and internal illustrations by Allan Stomann
Typeset in 14/18 Bembo by Helen Beard, ECJ Australia Pty Limited
Printed and bound in Australia by Griffin Press on 60gsm Bulky Paperback

6 5 4 3 2 1   05 06 07 08

AUTHOR'S NOTE

Selby rang me to tell me about some new great adventures — about being covered in chocolate, about changing the taste of Dry-Mouth Dog Biscuits, about making up a killer joke — and then he said, 'But I haven't told you the best part yet.'

And I said, 'Your life sounds like a complete shemozzle.'

'Hey, then let's call the book *Selby's Shemozzle*,' he said. 'I love that word! "Shemozzle" — what does it mean?'

'It's a mix-up, a muddle, a mess,' I said. 'A dog's breakfast.'

'A dog's breakfast? Like Dry-Mouth Dog Biscuits?'

'Well, not exactly,' I said. 'It's just that you always cause confusion. I know you don't try to.'

'Will kids know what a shemozzle is?' Selby asked.

'They will when they read the book,' I said. 'Now what about the "best part yet" that you were going to tell me?'

'Oh yes,' he said. 'I'm invisible.'

'You're *what*?'

'Invisible! I've disappeared. I'm gone. Actually, I'm not gone — I'm still here, only no one can see me.'

'Is that true?'

'Of course it's true. Would I lie to you?'

'How are you going to get visible again?'

'I'm not. I like being invisible. I think I'll stay this way.'

And that's when Selby told me his greatest adventure yet ... or at least, the first part of it.

Duncan Ball

CONTENTS

NOW YOU SEE ME

Hiya kids. It's me, the only talking
dog in Australia and, perhaps, the
world. **Now** do I have some great
stories to tell **you**! Read this
book and you'll **see** all the fantastic
things that happened to me. I
found a lot of money. Then I won
a lot of money. I gave away my
secret. I bit a hairy monster on
the bum. I met the only talking
cat in Australia (and, perhaps, the
world) and I became invisible
and —

I'd better not ruin it by telling
you too much about what happened
to **me**. So kick off your shoes
cos you're in for a cruise.
(I hope you like it.)

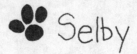 Selby

SELBY'S
SHEMOZZLE

Selby was lying on his mat in the Trifles' house when he heard a familiar voice.

'This tape has some of the jokes for my new show,' said Gary Gaggs, the Trifles' old friend and favourite comedian. 'Do you want to hear some?'

'I'd love to,' Mrs Trifle said.

'Me too!' Selby thought as Gary started the tape player. 'I just love this guy's jokes.'

'Okay, here goes ... A fellow goes to a doctor and the doctor listens to his chest and says, "There's something ticking in there." And the guy says, "I know, I swallowed a clock." And the doctor says, "Why didn't you tell me that

1

straightaway?" And the guy says, "Because I didn't want to alarm you."'

'Oh, I get it,' Selby thought. '*Alarm* you. It was an alarm clock. That's great!'

'I said to a friend of mine, I said, "Cheer up. Things could be worse." So he cheered up and, sure enough, things got worse. Woo woo woo!' Gary added, as he often did at the end of a joke. 'A burglar broke into my house last night. I pulled out a gun and said, "Take one more step and I'll let you have it!" He took another step so I let him have it. What was I going to do with that old gun anyway?'

'I don't get it,' Selby thought. '*Oh! Oh! Oh!* Now I do! He let him *have* it. He let him have *the gun*. Oh, Gary, that's great!'

'That's a good one, Gary,' Mrs Trifle said with a laugh.

'A mother says to her son, "I'm going to make you eat your words!" And the kid says, "How can you do that?" And she says, "We're having alphabet soup for lunch." Woo woo woo! But seriously, folks, an astronaut is about to step down onto the moon. A little green alien comes running up and says, "Go away! You can't land here!" And the astronaut says, "Why not?" So the alien says, "Because the moon is *full*." Woo woo woo! The other day I was in an art gallery and this lady said to a guard, "That painting over there of a woman is the ugliest painting I've ever seen!" And the guard said, "I hate to tell you this, lady, but that's not a painting — it's a mirror."'

'Oh, she was looking at herself!' Selby thought. 'This guy cracks me up. But I've got to keep from laughing or I'll give away my secret!'

'But seriously, folks,' Gary's tape continued, 'a girl bought a rubber piano. She wanted to play in a rubber band.'

Gary stopped the tape player.

'Do you like the jokes?' he asked.

'Yes, but that last one was terrible!' Mrs Trifle said with a laugh. 'By the way, is this show coming here, to Bogusville?'

'Are you kidding? They hate me here.'

'They don't hate you, Gary. They're just afraid you'll tell your killer joke 🐾 again. I'm so glad we didn't go to that show.'

🐾 *Paw note: Duncan mentioned this in the 'Author's Note' at the beginning of Selby's Side-Splitting Joke Book.* **S**

'Me too,' Selby thought.

'Don't remind me,' said Gary with a sigh. 'What a shemozzle. Half the audience landed in hospital from laughing too hard. And the rest of them ripped their pants. I couldn't even stop laughing myself.'

'You laughed at your own joke?'

'It was very, *very* funny. And I hadn't heard the punchline before.'

'What do you mean?'

'It's a strange thing, being a comedian,' Gary explained. 'Sometimes you're telling a joke and your mouth takes over. It's like it has a mind of its own.'

'A mind of its own?'

'Yes. I'd told that joke lots of times before, but this time, just when I was about to say the punchline, suddenly I said something that was a thousand times funnier. It turned into a killer joke. For weeks afterwards I laughed every time I thought of it. In the end I had to make a recording of the joke and just listen to it over and over again till it wore off.'

'I'm so glad I didn't hear it,' said Mrs Trifle. 'Speaking of your new show — are you going to tell that elephant and mouse joke? You told it to us once at dinner, remember?'

'No, I've never been able to make that joke work. I've changed it and changed it but it's still not funny enough.'

'Well, I thought it was sweet. Will you tell it now?'

'Tell it, Gary,' Selby thought. 'I liked it too.'

'Okay. An elephant and a mouse are walking down the street. The mouse says, "I hate being small. I'd love to be big like you." And the elephant says, "You could be big like me if you wanted to. Here's what you do. First find the nut of the jub–jub tree and bring it to me." "Is that all I have to do?" "Yes, but the nearest jub–jub tree is a long way away and the nuts are very heavy." "No problem," says the mouse, "I'll roll it back." And the elephant says, "You'll have to go through lion country." "I'll do it," says the mouse. "And you'll have to cross a river full of crocodiles." "No problem," the mouse says. So off the mouse goes . . .'

Selby listened as the elephant and mouse joke went on and on. Finally Gary got to the punchline: '"Okay," the elephant says, "so now we're both nuts but I'm still tall."'

'That's a lovely joke,' Mrs Trifle said.

'Thanks. But it didn't make you laugh.'

'It's just me. I'm not in a laughing mood. I'm too worried about the speech I have to give on the radio tomorrow.'

'What's it about?'

'I have to tell the people of Bogusville that they're going to close our hospital.'

'That's awful!'

'I know. The Health Department says that Bogusville is too small to have its own hospital. From now on, if anyone gets sick they'll have to go to Poshfield Hospital.'

'So why are you worried about your speech? It's not your fault they're closing the hospital.'

'I always get nervous when I talk on the radio. And when I get nervous I make mistakes.'

'Well, then,' Gary said, putting a blank tape into the tape player, 'record your speech till you get it right. Then give it to the radio station to play.'

'Gary, you're a genius!' said Mrs Trifle.

★ ★ ★

That afternoon, Mrs Trifle recorded her speech over and over again.

'She's almost got it right,' Selby thought, 'but listening to it is driving me nuts. I've got to get out of here.'

Selby left the house and went walking along Bogusville Creek, practising some of Gary's jokes in his best Gary Gaggs voice: 'But seriously, folks,' he said. 'A guy in a restaurant says to the waiter, "I can't eat this soup." The waiter says, "I'll get the manager." So the guy says to the manager, "I can't eat this soup." The manager says, "I'll get the owner." So the guy says to the owner, "I can't eat this soup." The owner says, "I'll get the cook." The guy says to the cook, "I can't eat this soup." The cook says, "Why not?" So the guy says, "Because I don't have a spoon." Woo woo woo!'

'It was funnier when Gary told it,' Selby thought. 'Now how did that elephant and mouse joke go? "An elephant and a mouse are walking down the street. The mouse says . . ."'

When Selby got to the end of the joke and was about to say Gary's punchline, something strange happened. It was as if Selby's mouth had a mind of its own. Suddenly a completely different punchline came out.

Selby stopped in his tracks. 'That is so incredibly funny,' he thought in the split second before he started laughing uncontrollably.

He doubled up and fell to the ground, pounding his paws in the dirt.

'That is *sooooooo* funny!' he cried. 'That's the funniest joke I've ever heard — and I made it up myself! I'm a real comedian! *Oh! Oh! Oh!* My tummy is hurting from laughing.'

Selby shrieked with laughter again and rolled on the ground. Tears streamed down his face. For what seemed like hours he shouted and groaned and writhed in helpless laughter. Finally he picked himself up, his throat raw and sore, but he was still laughing faintly.

'I have to go home,' he gasped, 'or the Trifles will worry.'

With weak and wobbly legs, Selby dragged himself back towards home. The sun was setting behind Gumboot Mountain. Finally his laughter stopped — and then . . .

'Oh, no!' he thought. 'It doesn't look like a gumboot at all! It looks like an elephant! *Oh! Oh! Oh!* The mouse and the elephant!'

Once again Selby found himself on the ground screeching with laughter. By the time he got home he'd finally stopped.

Three times that night Selby woke himself up with his own laughter. In the morning he could hear Mrs Trifle talking on the telephone.

'I don't know what you heard,' she was telling someone, 'but it can't have been an escaped hyena, because Bogusville Zoo has never *had* a hyena. But don't worry, the police are looking into it.'

'It was me!' Selby thought. 'I have to get that joke out of my head.'

As soon as the Trifles left the house, Selby dashed to the tape recorder and turned Mrs Trifle's tape around.

'I'll do what Gary did. I'll record the joke and listen to it till I'm sick of it.'

Selby recorded the joke using his best Gary Gaggs voice, to make it as funny as possible. Then he played the tape over and over again. After a while his laughter stopped.

'I'm cured!' Selby thought. 'And just in time. Here come the Trifles!'

Selby quickly turned the tape around again and lay down.

'Time to catch up on my sleep,' he thought.

Hours later, Selby awoke to the sound of Dr Trifle's voice.

'You should be on right now,' Dr Trifle said, turning on the radio.

'And now,' the radio announcer said, 'we have the very important message from Mayor Trifle that I've been telling you about. Here goes.'

But the voice that came on the radio wasn't Mrs Trifle's.

'An elephant and a mouse are walking down the street,' it said. 'The mouse says, "I hate being small. I'd love to be big like you . . ."'

'That's not me,' Mrs Trifle said. 'It's Gary Gaggs. They're playing the wrong tape.'

'Oh, no,' Selby groaned in his head. 'That's not Gary — it's me telling Gary's joke with my killer punchline! They're playing the wrong side of the tape!'

'Should we ring the radio station?' asked Dr Trifle.

'No, no,' Mrs Trifle said. 'Not till the joke is over. It's a cute joke. It'll put everyone in a good mood for my announcement.'

'I can't stand it,' Selby screamed in his brain. 'Everyone in Bogusville is listening! I've got to get out of here!'

It was a sad and lonely dog who walked along the streets of Bogusville, watching as people staggered, screaming with laughter, from their houses. And all around town there was hideous howling like the sound of a herd of escaped hyenas. Selby watched helplessly as people crawled along the footpaths, gasping for breath, and laughing ambulance officers tried to lift people onto stretchers.

'Oh woe woe woe,' Selby groaned as a jogger, blinded by his own tears, ran off the side of a bridge and straight into Bogusville Creek. 'What a shemozzle! And poor Gary is going to get the blame. I'll never ever think up another joke as long as I live. Oh, this is the saddest day of my life.'

Fortunately, no one died because of Selby's killer joke. A few people tumbled out of bed or off toilets, and Melanie Mildew fell out of a tree while she was picking apples. Postie Paterson laughed so much that he cried and for days he delivered the wrong mail to the wrong houses. Mrs Trifle laughed so hard that she started hiccupping and couldn't stop. And Aunt Jetty swallowed her false teeth. But no one was badly hurt — which was lucky, because the doctors and nurses at the hospital were laughing too hard to help anyone.

A month later, when Selby was still feeling guilty, he heard Mrs Trifle say to Dr Trifle, 'Good news — they've decided not to close Bogusville Hospital after all.'

'Why not?'

'Because it was suddenly very busy. Do you realise that three thousand patients went to hospital last month?'

'Really? Oh yes,' Dr Trifle said with a laugh, 'the joke injuries.'

'So they're keeping the hospital open, after all!' Selby thought. 'That's great! And to think it's all because of me. I'm a hero!'

'And to think,' said Mrs Trifle, 'it's all because of Gary. When he gets back he'll be a hero.'

'Did you see that?' Dr Trifle said. 'Selby was lying there as quiet as a mouse and suddenly his ears went up. It was almost as if he was listening to us.'

'Did you say *a mouse*?' Mrs Trifle asked, a smile spreading across her face. 'That reminds me of the elephant and mouse joke.'

'Me too!' Dr Trifle hooted with laughter. 'Oh, the elephant and the mouse! Oh, that's so funny!'

'I'm getting out of here before I start laughing too,' Selby thought. 'This has gone beyond a joke!'

Author's note: See the whole of Selby's killer joke in Appendix 1 on page 162.

SELBY'S STASH
OF CASH

'This is very strange,' Mrs Trifle said to Dr Trifle. 'I thought I'd spent all my money, but I just found a new twenty-dollar note in my wallet. It's the third time this week it's happened. Have you been putting money in there?'

'No. Come to think of it, yesterday I was sure I'd spent my last ten dollars, but today I saw that I still have twenty dollars left.'

'Well, either we're getting very forgetful,' Mrs Trifle said, 'or we have a guardian angel who's giving us money.'

'You do,' Selby thought, 'and I'm him — guardian angel Selby. It's so nice to be able to

15

give the Trifles a little back in return for all their kindness to me.'

Suddenly there was music and wavy lines in the air as Selby thought back to how all this had started, that moment when the money had magically appeared . . .

It was a happy dog who strolled along the banks of Bogusville Creek when suddenly — 'Ouch!' — he stubbed his toe on a half-buried biscuit tin.

'A half-buried biscuit tin,' he thought as he dug it out of the ground. 'That can mean only one thing — biscuits! And not those horrible Dry-Mouth Dog Biscuits, but scrummy people biscuits!'

Selby prised off the lid and his heart sank.

'No biscuits. Just a bit of money.'

For one terrible second Selby thought of burying the tin again.

'Hang on. Did I say *money*? Yes, I think I did. Money! It's a pile of twenty-dollar notes! A stack of smackeroos! A dollop of dough! A lovely mass of moolah! *Yippppeeeee*! I'm rich!'

Selby started to throw the money up in the

air, the way people do in movies, but then thought better of it.

'Well, it isn't that much,' he thought, thumbing through it. 'I wonder who could have hidden it here? Oh well, finders keepers.'

Selby lay on his mat that night wondering what to buy.

'I can't think of anything I need,' he thought. 'A new bowl? A new mat? The Trifles give me everything I need. Hey! That's it! I'll give it to the Trifles. They're always short of cash.'

And so it was that Selby got the idea to secretly slip a little bit of money into the Trifles' wallets every night when they were sleeping.

'I'll stash the rest of the cash in that mess in the corner of Dr Trifle's workroom. That would be the last place anyone would look for anything.'

The wavy lines came and went away, leaving a slightly smiling guardian angel dog lying happily in the Trifles' lounge room once again.

'Goodness me, look at the time!' Mrs Trifle exclaimed. 'Postie Paterson and Melanie Mildew are due at any minute to get some of my bread dough.'

'Everyone loves your new recipe. You ought to open a bakery,' said Dr Trifle. 'Did you just hear something?'

'Yes, there's some sort of commotion in the street.'

Mrs Trifle opened the curtains to see a huge group of police running down the street. Behind them were police cars and police vans and police helicopters were circling overhead.

'It's some kind of raid!' Dr Trifle exclaimed. 'They must be after a gang of hardened criminals.'

'Uh-oh,' Selby thought as the police turned into the Trifles' driveway. 'They must have the wrong address! This is scary!'

'Come out with your hands up, Mayor Trifle!' the police captain yelled. 'We've got the house surrounded! And don't try any funny business.'

Dr and Mrs Trifle looked at each other.

'What'll we do?' said Dr Trifle.

'We'd better do as they say,' Mrs Trifle answered.

Mrs Trifle opened the door and stepped out with her hands in the air. Dr Trifle followed closely behind.

'If it's about that overdue library book,' she said, 'I can explain everything.'

'It's not about overdue library books,' the police captain said. 'I think you know what it's about — funny money.'

'Funny money?' Mrs Trifle said. 'What on earth do you mean?'

'You know perfectly well what I mean, Mayor Trifle. You've been caught passing party paper. You know — crazy cash, laughing lucre.'

'Crazy cash?' Mrs Trifle said.

'Phoney money, Mrs Trifle. You made a big mistake when you spent a fake twenty-dollar note at the supermarket this morning.'

'Fake twenty?' Mrs Trifle·said.

'Fake twenty?' Dr Trifle said, taking a twenty-dollar note out of his wallet and looking at it.

'Aha! There's another one!' cried the captain, grabbing it out of Dr Trifle's hand. 'So you're in this together.'

'Gulp,' thought Selby. 'It's from my stash! It's all fake money! What have I done?'

'Surely you don't think that *we* are making phoney money,' Dr Trifle said. 'Why, we're completely honest! We've never done anything wrong in our lives. Well, except my wife keeping that library book a bit longer than she should have.'

'Don't try that innocence nonsense with me, Dr Trifle. I know you people who forge money. I know how you live. I know how you think. You're the sneakiest criminals in the world. You pretend to be nice people. You're good to your neighbours. You're polite. You give money to charities. You're the sort of people who everyone *thinks* are honest. When you give one of your fake banknotes to someone in a shop, they don't hold it up to the light or look at it carefully, because they trust you.'

'B–B–But we're not forgers,' Mrs Trifle said.

'They're certainly not!' Selby thought.

'Which is what you people always say,' said the captain. 'You deny everything. That's why I know you're guilty.'

'You know we're guilty because we say we're innocent?' Dr Trifle asked.

'Exactly!'

'Then we're crooks,' Dr Trifle said. 'We're forgers. We're guilty. What do you say to that?'

'Aha! So you admit it! I knew you'd crack. This is the quickest confession I've ever got.'

'No, no, he was kidding!' Mrs Trifle said. 'We have nothing to hide. Go ahead, search the house.'

'Yeah,' Selby thought. 'Go ahead and search the house. Wait — what am I saying? No! *Don't* search the house!'

'Is this a trick?' the captain said. 'Forgers never hide the money in their own houses. They bury it in biscuit tins so that if anyone finds it they don't know whose it is. But go ahead, boys, you heard the mayor — search the house. Maybe you'll find the printing plates they use to print the money.'

'Oh, woe woe,' Selby thought. 'Why didn't I just leave that money where I found it?'

'I've been watching this town for ten years, since you started spending your funny money,' said the captain. 'You stopped last December, but you didn't fool me. I knew that sooner or later the Laughing Lady would show up again.'

'The Laughing Lady?' asked Mrs Trifle.

'Here's a proper twenty-dollar note and here's one of yours,' the captain said. 'Yours is almost a perfect copy. But when you made your printing plates, you made one tiny mistake. Look at the lady in the picture — you made her mouth curve up a tiny bit. It looks like she's laughing.'

'How interesting,' Dr Trifle said, studying the banknotes.

One of the police officers came out of the house.

'We found it,' he said. 'A whole stack of Laughing Ladies hidden under some things in the workroom. It was the first place we looked.'

'Okay, Dr and Mrs Trifle,' the captain said. 'Now tell us where you've hidden the printing plates. Those won't be buried in the ground because they'd rust. But we know they're here somewhere.'

'What's going on here?' cried Melanie Mildew, making her way through the police line, followed by Postie Paterson. 'What are you doing to the Trifles?'

'We're arresting them for making money.'

'You can't arrest people for making money,' Melanie said. 'They make plenty of money. So what? They've been doing it for years.'

'Just as I thought.'

'You don't understand,' Postie Paterson said. 'The Trifles are the most honest people in the whole town.'

'And what brings you two here?' the captain asked. 'Are you part of their gang?'

'Gang?!' Melanie exclaimed. 'We're not part of any gang. Mrs Trifle said she'd give us some dough today.'

'Some dough? So you were helping them pass off the Laughing Ladies.'

'I don't know what you're talking about,' said Postie. 'It was bread. Mrs Trifle makes lots of bread.'

'I've heard enough,' the police captain said. 'Take the Trifles away, guys. And take these two away for questioning as well.'

'Oh, woe woe woe,' Selby said to himself. 'I was only trying to help and I created a terrible shemozzle. I should have suspected there was something wrong with that money. It was all too easy.'

Selby watched as police officers searched the house from floor to ceiling, even cutting open mattresses and ripping pillows apart, trying to find the plates.

'They won't find anything, because there's nothing to find,' Selby thought. 'But the Trifles could go to jail for years and years and years just because they had my stash of cash.'

Selby blinked back a tear.

'I know,' Selby thought. 'I'll write a letter to the cops and tell them what really happened. But I won't sign it so they won't know who I am.'

Selby thought again.

'That's silly. They won't believe it. I guess I'm just going to have to go to the police station and tell them. I'll be giving away my secret (*sniff*) and I may have to go to jail (*sniff sniff*) but at least they'll have to let the Trifles and Melanie and Postie go.'

'Hey! Look what I found under the house!' one of the police officers said, holding up Selby's dog suit disguise. 'These people are weird.'

Selby started out the door just as another police officer ran a metal detector up and down the walls.

'Now hang on,' Selby thought. 'Somewhere in Bogusville there must be the real forger. All I have to do is find him and then call the cops. Hmmm,' Selby hmmmed. 'Where do I start? I'll make a list of the most honest, helpful and friendly people in Bogusville.'

It was a cunning dog that crept into the Trifles' study and opened the drawer marked 'Bogusville Council'. In it was a file folder called 'Awards'.

Selby read through the list of all the people who had been given awards for tidiness, cleanliness and all the other nesses that Bogusville gave awards for.

One name came up time after time — Mavis Deeds.

'Oh, isn't that sweet that she got all those awards,' Selby thought. 'She was so nice. I used to see her walking along Bogusville Creek. She always stopped to pat me. It couldn't be her. Hang on! What am I saying? Maybe it *was* her. I used to see her near where I found the biscuit tin. No, she was too nice. But hang on again! She's got to be my first suspect just *because* she was so nice. But wait — she can't be the one because she died last December.'

Selby looked down his list of names again.

'She died last December!' he said out loud (and almost *too* out loud). 'That's when the money stopped. It was her! It absolutely had to be her! I wonder if that old house of hers has been sold yet?'

'Hey! Who nicked my metal detector?' a police officer cried. 'Come on, guys, a joke's a joke! Give it back.'

It was a window-lifting dog that climbed into Mavis Deeds' empty house and scanned its walls with a borrowed metal detector. And it was a very happy dog that heard the *beep beep beep* on his headphones.

Selby grabbed a (borrowed) hammer and with a *crash thump bang* made a hole in the wall.

'The plates!' he yelled. 'I've found them!'

'Thank heavens someone found those money-printing plates and called the police,' Mrs Trifle said to Dr Trifle when they got home. 'And to think that the forger was that sweet little old lady, Mavis Deeds. She was the very last person I would have suspected.'

'Do you really think that was her real name?' Dr Trifle asked.

'Why not?'

'She never married, did she?'

'No, I don't believe so.'

'And she always called herself Miss Deeds.'

'Miss Deeds?' Mrs Trifle said. 'Oh, I get it. *Mis*deeds are *bad* deeds, aren't they? I guess that was her little joke on us.'

'So she,' Selby thought as he curled up for a nap, 'was the Laughing Lady after all.'

SELBY AND THE CHOCOLATE FACTORY

'There's been a real shemozzle at Hippity Hop,' Dr Trifle said.

'A shemozzle?' asked Mrs Trifle.

'Yes — the bunnies are coming out funny.'

'Hippity Hop? Funny bunnies? I don't understand.'

'I'm afraid it's trouble with my EBM.'

'You must be talking about one of your inventions,' said Mrs Trifle. 'Would that be your Extra Bouncy Mattress? Or maybe it's your Electronic Burp Maker.'

'No, it's the *Easter Bunny Machine* I invented for Trudy Truffle to use in her Hippity Hop Chocolate Shop. She already had a machine that made little Easter bunnies. I changed it so it could make very big Easter bunnies. Only it's gone out of control. I have to get over there and fix it.'

'Remember that Willy and Billy are coming for lunch,' said Mrs Trifle. 'On the way back could you pick up something for dessert?'

'Like what?'

'Oh, anything. Maybe some apple pie.'

'Okay. I might take Selby with me. He's been stuck in the house all day.'

Selby's ears shot up.

'Oh, yummy!' he squealed in his brain. 'I love chocolate. It's my absolutely fave thing after peanut prawns. Maybe Trudy will give me a bunny.'

'Don't take Selby,' Mrs Trifle said. 'He might eat some chocolate.'

'What's wrong with that?'

'It's very bad for dogs — and cats. If they eat enough it can kill them.' 🐾

🐾 *Paw note: It's true. Never give your dog or cat chocolate.*

S

29

'But we used to give him chocolate cake, remember? It didn't hurt him then.'

'I didn't know about chocolate and dogs then.'

'But I've eaten tonnes of chocolate,' Selby thought as he crept outside. He quietly opened the car door and hid in the back. 'I'm going. I'm sure a little bit of chockie won't hurt me — I'm not like other dogs. And then I'll stay away from the house till the terrible twins have gone.'

Trudy Truffle, the owner and Chief Chocolate Chef of the Hippity Hop Chocolate Shop, was waiting at the door when Dr Trifle drove up.

'Thank goodness you're here!' she said. 'This is a disaster! It's a catastrophe! The bunnies aren't bunnies, they're monsters!'

Dr Trifle followed Trudy into the back of the shop, where he saw a terrible sight — huge dripping bunny monsters were coming along the production line.

Selby snuck out of the car and came through the back door.

'Sheeeesh!' Selby gasped. 'Those faces! Those mouths wide open and dripping chocolate!

They're bunny zombies! bunnies from beyond the grave! No wonder Trudy's upset.'

'What am I going to do?' Trudy asked. 'No one will buy these.'

'Maybe you could save them till Halloween.'

'They're even too horrible for Halloween! Besides, Easter is only a week away and people want their chocolate bunnies now. Oh, Dr Trifle, I wish I hadn't let you change the machine.'

'Hmmm,' Dr Trifle hmmmed. 'Are you recycling the bad bunnies?'

'Yes. They all get chopped up and melted down again, like this.'

Trudy Truffle picked up a monster bunny and threw it into the Bunny Chopper and Melter.

'Good, then nothing's wasted,' Dr Trifle said as they climbed up to the chocolate vat.

They watched as two mechanical arms shot out in front of them, clamping a metal mould into the chocolate and then placing a big bunny on the conveyor belt.

Dr Trifle dipped a finger into the chocolate and licked it. 'This chocolate is delicious.'

'It's my new secret recipe. Everyone loves it.'

'New recipe? Does it have more oil in it?'

'Why, yes, it does.'

'Aha! That's the problem!' Dr Trifle exclaimed. 'You've made the chocolate softer. The bunnies are too runny.'

'Then I guess I'll have to go back to the old recipe.'

'No, don't do that. I'll just make the cooling tube cooler. That should fix things.'

As Trudy Truffle and Dr Trifle climbed down the ladder at the front of the vat, Selby crept up the one at the back.

'Dr Trifle is brilliant!' he thought. 'Two minutes and he's solved the problem.'

Selby ducked as the grabber arms swung around and splashed down into the chocolate, lifting out another fully formed bunny.

'What a heavenly smell!' he thought as he leant over the rim of the vat towards the melted chocolate. 'Oh, I just have to have a little tasty-wasty.'

Selby leant way over, had a lick of chocolate and then pulled back just in time to miss the grabber arms.

'Sheesh, that was close!' he thought. 'But that chocolate is sooooo yummy!'

Selby turned to go and then stopped.

'Maybe one more little lick.'

Once again Selby leant way over and licked. Over the rim of the vat he could see Dr Trifle turning a knob on the side of the machine.

'I'd better get out of here before they see me,' Selby thought.

He leaned over for one last lick, but this time he could feel his paws losing their grip and sliding towards the chocolate.

'Uh-oh!' he thought as he struggled to stand up. 'I'm going in!'

In a second, Selby had fallen deep into the chocolate.

'I can't swim!' he screamed in his brain. 'I'll be the first dog ever to drown in chocolate!'

Selby bobbed to the surface, gasping for breath and swallowing gobs of chocolate. He looked up and saw the huge grabber arms coming towards him. 'They're going to get me!' he thought. Suddenly the grabber clamped around him and dropped him onto the conveyor belt.

'Oh no!' Selby squealed in his brain. 'Help! Let me out of here!'

Selby reached up to pull the chocolate away from his face, but as he did, the extra-cold air in the cooling tube hit him, hardening the chocolate.

'I can't move,' he thought. 'And I can't breathe!'

Selby tried to open his mouth to lick away the chocolate, but his jaw wouldn't budge.

'This is the end,' he thought. 'I'm a chunk of chockie! I'm a slab of sweet! I've been bunnied! I'm a done dog!'

Selby's life flashed in front of him. He remembered when he was watching TV years ago and he suddenly understood everything the people on TV were saying. 🐾 He remembered teaching himself how to talk people-talk, and he remembered the day he decided to keep it a secret.

'The Trifles were (*sniff*) wonderful to me,' he whimpered. 'They're the kindest most loving

🐾 *Paw note: See the first story, 'Selby's Secret', in the book* Selby's Secret. **S**

34

people in the (*sniff*) world. Now I've gone and got myself chocolate-coated — and I'm going to (*sniff*) die.'

Selby could feel the hot tears in his eyes as he thought of the great times he'd had with the Trifles. He blinked, and then he blinked some more. From the darkness inside the chocolate, Selby saw a light that grew brighter and brighter.

'It's over,' he thought. 'I'm on my way to heaven.'

Selby blinked and blinked again.

'Now hang on,' he thought. 'My tears are dissolving the chocolate! Hey! I can see!'

Selby wiggled his face loose from the inside of the chocolate.

'And now I can breathe! The air is coming through the eye holes! And I can hear! Well, just a tiny bit.'

'The bunnies are okay now,' Selby heard Trudy say. 'Ooops!' she said suddenly, seeing Selby. 'Another bad one. Strange — this one looks more like a dog than a bunny.'

'There are bound to be a few duds,' Dr Trifle said, picking Selby up. 'I'll just chuck this one in the chopper-upper.'

Selby barked as loudly as he could, considering he was barking through chocolate and he couldn't open his mouth.

'Did you hear something?' Dr Trifle asked.

'You mean like a dog barking?'

'Something like that.'

'No, I didn't.'

Once again Dr Trifle was about to drop Selby into the spinning blades.

'No! No!' Selby screamed out loud in plain English as he saw the whirring blades coming closer. 'Don't mince me! I'm not some bodgie bunny! I'm Selby, the only talking dog in Australia and, perhaps, the world! And I don't want to die!'

Dr Trifle turned to Trudy Truffle.

'Did you say something?'

'No, I thought you did. I thought you said something about pie.'

'Pie? That reminds me — I've got to take home some dessert.'

'How about some chocolate?' Trudy said. 'Why don't you take home a nice big Easter bunny?'

'Oh, no, I couldn't possibly do that.'

'Yes, you could,' Selby thought. 'You could!'

'I guess I could take this one,' Dr Trifle said.

'Yes, yes, take me! Take me!' Selby squealed in his brain.

'No, don't take that ugly one. Take a nice one.'

'No! Take me! Take the ugly one!'

'Oh, I couldn't possibly take one that you could sell.'

'That's right!' Selby thought. 'Take me! *Please* take me.'

'It's okay,' Trudy said. 'Drop it in the chopper and it'll be melted down and you'll have a nice new one in a couple of minutes.'

'No, I won't be melted,' Selby whimpered. 'I'll be all chopped up. I'll ruin the chocolate!'

'Something tells me I should take this one,' Dr Trifle said. 'Besides, it's only for my nephews. They won't notice what it looks like.'

Meanwhile Willy and Billy had finished their lunch and were running round the Trifles' house.

'Where's that stinky doggy?' Willy yelled.

'If you mean Selby,' Mrs Trifle said, 'I don't know. He does have a way of disappearing just before you boys appear. Sometimes I think he knows you're coming.'

'Look!' Billy screamed as Dr Trifle came through the door. 'It's a Easter ... a Easter ...'

'An Easter bunny,' Dr Trifle said. 'Only this one came out a bit wonky.'

'It looks like a doggy!' Willy screeched. 'Can we eat him? Can we? Can we? Can we?'

'Settle down,' Mrs Trifle said. 'Take the bunny out to the backyard and you may each have a bit. I don't want you eating too much or you'll make yourselves sick. And don't make a mess — do you hear?'

'Yes, Auntie,' the boys both said at once.

Selby looked out through the eye holes as Willy and Billy carried him away.

'How am I going to get out of here without anyone noticing?' he thought. 'What am I saying? How am I going to get out of here *at all*!'

For the next few minutes, Selby could feel bits of chocolate being broken off him.

'Eat more, kids,' he thought. 'Come on.'

'Hey, Willy,' Billy said. 'Do bunnies have tails?'

'Of course they do, Billy.'

'I know that, Willy, but do they have big long ones? Cos this one has a big long tail.'

'That's not a tail, dummy.'

'Yes, it is! It's coming out of his bum, see? And don't call me a dummy, you stupid-head!'

'I'm going to kill you, you stink-face!'

'And I'm going to kill you, too, dumbo!'

Selby listened as Willy and Billy chased each other all around the backyard. And as they did, he could feel his chocolate coating getting softer and softer in the sun. He took a deep breath and then let it out again.

'It's no good. The chocolate won't break. It's still too hard. I'll just have to wait till it melts some more.'

'Hey, Billy!' Willy said. 'Let's push the bunny in the pool.'

'Okay, Willy.'

Willy and Billy dragged Selby towards the swimming pool.

'They're going to drown me!' Selby thought. 'I've got to get out of here!' He started yelling. 'Let me go, you brats! Don't you dare throw me in the pool!'

With Selby right at the edge of the pool, Willy and Billy suddenly stopped.

'Do Easter bunnies talk, Willy?'

'No.'

'This one talked, Willy.'

'Did not.'

'Did so.'

'Didn't!'

'Did!'

'*You're stupid!*' Willy screamed.

'*No, I'm not! You are!*' Billy screamed back.

Just then Selby took his deepest breath ever, breaking the chocolate around him into hundreds of pieces. Willy and Billy stopped screaming.

'It's the dog!' Willy cried. 'It's him! Auntie! Come quick!'

'What *are* you boys talking about?' Mrs Trifle said, walking out into the yard. 'Look at the mess you've made! You've spread chocolate all over the yard! And you promised you wouldn't!'

'We didn't do it, Auntie — it was him!' Willy said, pointing to Selby.

'And look what you've done to poor Selby! You've put chocolate all through his fur. That was cruel!'

'It's not my fault!' Willy bawled.

'I didn't do it!' Billy cried. 'The doggy did it! He was in the chocolate! Honest!'

'You're very naughty boys,' Mrs Trifle said. 'I'm going to ring your mother right now and she can come and take you home.'

'Isn't life wonderful?' Selby thought. 'The brats got the blame for something they didn't even do for a change.' He wandered over to a bush and settled down for a well-earned nap. 'Mrs Trifle was right. Chocolate is dangerous for dogs — well, it was for this dog, anyway.'

THE SHEMOZZLE BIRD

Of all the birds of which I've heard,
The worst is the Shemozzle Bird.
Even scientists confess —
This bird is a disgusting mess!

Its head is bald, its feathers tatty,
Everything about it's ratty,
It picks up garbage all day long,
While giving off an awful pong.

It fills its nest with vile scum,
Like chunks of spat-out chewing gum,
A rotting fish, some hair, a caper,
And even pre-owned toilet paper.

Most birdies like to sing and chirp,
But this one likes to sit and burp.
While other birds have gone extinct,
Forget the *ex* — this bird just stinks.

So if you ever hear its cry
Above you on a branch nearby,
Don't stick around, don't hang about,
And don't look up — just get out!

SYLVIA'S SECRET

'That must be a very funny book,' Dr Trifle said. 'You've been giggling away for ages.'

'It is,' Mrs Trifle said, wiping away her tears. 'It's a children's book called *Sylvia's Secret*. It's about a cat that can talk but she's keeping it a secret.'

Selby's ears shot up.

'It sounds a bit like those books about what's-his-name, the talking dog,' Dr Trifle said.

'More than just a bit,' Selby thought. '*Sylvia's Secret* sounds exactly like the books about me!'

'Only this cat lives with the author and talks

to her all the time,' Mrs Trifle said. 'That's what she claims, anyway.'

'Hmmm,' Dr Trifle hmmmed. 'So why are you reading it?'

'Because the author of the book, Fiona Fullstop, has asked me to launch it.'

'Launch it? Will it float?'

'No, no — a launch is just a party they have when a book is published. This launch is going to be at the Bogusville Bijou Theatre and I've been asked to talk about the book.'

'I've never heard of the author.'

'She lives in the city, but she came to Bogusville once and loved it. She said that we're warm and friendly people.'

'Well, that's true.'

'There are going to be newspaper, radio and TV people from all around the world at the launch because Fiona is going to bring her talking cat with her.'

'She is?' Selby thought. 'A *real* talking cat?'

'She is?' Dr Trifle asked. 'Is that possible?'

'I don't think so,' said Mrs Trifle. 'I suspect she just said it to get the press to come along. When the cat doesn't talk Fiona will say that

Sylvia is just too shy today. She'll say, "What's wrong, Sylvia, has the cat got your tongue?" and make a joke of it.'

'Or maybe,' Dr Trifle added, 'she'll say that Sylvia can't talk right now because her throat's sore from talking too much.'

'It doesn't really matter,' Mrs Trifle said. 'It's just a bit of harmless fun to get publicity for the book.'

As soon as the Trifles were out of the house, Selby picked up the copy of *Sylvia's Secret*.

'Harmless fun, my paw,' he thought. 'The woman's a copier. And that cat is a copycat cat. She's just trying to get the kids to read her books instead of mine!'

Selby opened the book to a scribbly page at the beginning. It said:

Hi, my gorgeous and cute little readers. Guess who is writing these words? It's me, and — would you believe it? — I'm a cat! A real, live honest-to-goodness talking and reading and writing cat. My owner, the wonderful and beautiful Fiona, and I have been keeping it a secret that I know how to talk. I tell her my stories and she writes them down. But you're allowed to know — just you.

I've had lots of great adventures and they're all in this book. But my best times are when Fiona makes me my favourite food — prawns cooked with cashew nuts — and we just sit around watching DVDs and talking. Happy reading from your favourite little kitty witty, Sylvia.

'What a rip-off!' Selby said. 'And I'll bet the stories are rubbish. They're just made-up stories, not like my *real* ones.'

Selby read the first story. In it Sylvia went on a bus trip by herself wearing her disguise, a cat suit.

'That was a good one,' Selby admitted. 'I liked the bit where someone stepped on the tail of the cat suit and it ripped open and nearly gave away her secret.'

In the next story Sylvia drove a tank and almost started a war. And in the third one Sylvia took cooking lessons but she burnt the toast and the building caught fire.

'Hey, that last one was really funny. I loved the way she had them throw custard pies on the fire to put it out. This little kitty witty is a very witty little kitty. The book may be a rip-off but at least it's a good rip-off.'

Selby read on till he'd finished the book.

'The best story of all,' he thought, 'was the one where she feels lonely and she falls in love with another cat — only it turns out to be a robot cat. Poor Sylvia. That really made my little heart go pitter-patter. She sounds lovely.'

Selby lay there trying to imagine what it would be like if Sylvia lived with him and the Trifles.

'We could keep it a secret and only talk when they were out of the house,' he thought, 'or when we went on long walks together. And we could listen to my *The Screaming Mimis* CD and watch the DVD of *Hearthwarm Heath*. Hey, and I could teach her salsa dancing! It's so sad that she's not real.' Selby blinked back a tear as he looked at the cartoon picture of Sylvia on the cover of the book.

He puckered up and gave her a big kiss.

'Now, hang on!' he thought. 'Why do I think she can't be a real talking cat? I mean, I'm a real talking dog. Oh, Sylvia, I've got to know if you're real!'

* * *

It was a light-footed dog that tiptoed into the back of the Bogusville Bijou Theatre and hid behind a rack of clothes in the dressing room. Sitting in front of a mirror was a blonde woman powdering her cheeks.

'That's her!' Selby thought. 'That's Fiona Fullstop, the author. She's not nearly as pretty as the picture in the book, but I can still tell it's her. So where is Sylvia?'

Sitting next to Fiona was a short, plump woman.

'Are you nervous?' the woman asked.

'Of course I'm nervous, Davina. I hate these things. I'm a writer, not a talker. By the way, where is everyone?'

'Most of Bogusville is out there and the mayor is on her way.'

'Forget them — I want TV cameras! I want reporters from newspapers and magazines from around the world! This should be huge!'

'Well, we do have a reporter from the *Bogusville Banner*.'

'The *Bogusville Banner*?!' Fiona cried. 'I've never heard of the *Bogusville Banner*!'

'And there's someone from Radio OK4U.'

'Radio OK4U? Is that a joke? I'm about to show off a real talking cat! The whole world should be here! What kind of a shemozzle is this?'

'I'm sorry, Fiona, but I did tell them. Maybe they just didn't believe it.'

'WHAAAAATTTT?' Fiona Fullstop shrieked. 'Are they calling me a liar? You believe me, don't you?'

'Well, yes, of course. I do love your book. It's just that ... you know ... I've never actually heard Sylvia speak. No one's ever heard her except you. And, quite frankly, some people think you just got the idea from the books about Selby, the talking dog.'

'Selby? But he's just a made-up dog!' Fiona cried. 'A dog could never talk! Dogs are stupid. Cats are smart.'

'I could tell you a thing or two,' Selby thought. 'Now where is this Sylvia? Where are you hiding her?'

'Don't you worry, Davina,' Fiona said, 'Sylvia will talk today — although she *is* feeling a bit low.

And her throat is very sore from talking so much recently. By the way, where have you put her?'

'She's just in the next room.'

Selby crept out from between the hanging clothes and into the room next door, quietly closing the door.

'What an awful woman! Hey, there's Sylvia,' he thought, seeing the small cat box on the floor. 'She's gorgeous! Such silky fur and what a delicate face. And those big eyes. Just looking at her makes my legs go all rubbery. I've got to make sure I don't scare her.'

Selby moved closer to the cat box.

'Hi, Sylvia,' he whispered. 'Please don't be frightened. I'm not going to hurt you. I think you know me — my name is Selby. You've read the books about me, haven't you?'

Sylvia stood up and rubbed against the bars of the cage. Selby could feel his heart beating faster at the sound of Sylvia's purring.

'Don't worry, I'm not a trick dog or a robot like the one in your book. I'm the real thing,' he said. 'You understand me, don't you? Here, have a sniff and you'll know I'm not just a toy.'

Selby pressed his face against the bars. Sylvia purred louder and then gave him a big lick that sent shivers up his spine.

'Oh, you are *sooooooo* gorgeous,' Selby sighed. 'I've read *Sylvia's Secret*. It's a wonderful book. I just loved everything about it. By the time I finished reading it, I knew that it was all true and that you were a real talking cat. I just had to find you.'

Selby pushed against the bars again and felt the warmth of Sylvia's soft fur. He thought of the times he and Sylvia would have together, talking and laughing together and comparing peanut prawns and cashew prawns.

'I've never had cashew prawns,' Selby said, 'but if you like them I know I'll love them. Have you ever tried peanut prawns?'

Selby waited for an answer, but Sylvia was silent.

'Trust me, Sylvia,' he said. 'And let me warn you about talking to everyone here today. It could be the biggest mistake you ever make. I haven't told anyone about my secret because I'm afraid that if it gets out it would ruin my life forever. I think you ought to think very carefully about this too.'

Another tingle went through him as Sylvia's eyes met his.

'People with cameras will be poking them in the windows of your house,' Selby warned. 'They'll be knocking on your door in the middle of the night to get your autograph. And you'll have to be very careful that no one catnaps you.'

Sylvia sat staring silently at Selby. She opened her mouth, as if about to speak, only to close it again.

'I know it's hard when you've only ever talked to Fiona,' said Selby, 'but you can trust me. Honest. And I've got a plan, Sylv. I'm going to open your cage and we will go away together. What do you think?'

'Miaow.'

'Oh Sylvie, Sylvie, Sylvie,' Selby pleaded. 'Please don't do this to me. We can both speak our own languages — we know that. But if we're going to make this friendship work, we'll have to talk people-talk. Say something. Give me a sign, any sign.'

'Miaow miaow,' Sylvia miaowed, this time more softly than ever.

Selby felt his legs begin to buckle under him as he looked at the beautiful creature in front of him. Then suddenly he remembered when he'd fallen in love with Lulu🐾 and how he'd been fooled by a robot. And he remembered the disaster that happened when he fell in love with the famous actress Bonnie Blake.🐾🐾 And then

🐾 *Paw note: See 'Selby in Love' in the book* Selby Screams.

🐾🐾 *See 'Selby Lovestruck' in the book* Selby Snowbound.

S

the disappointment when he fell in love with the beautiful Afghan Equity. 🐾

Suddenly Selby straightened up.

'Okay, Sylvia, I can see you're not going to talk to me. Maybe you don't trust me or maybe you're shy. Or maybe your throat is too sore from lots of talking. But I have to know if you can understand me, so I'm going to tell you a joke. If you understand it, you'll laugh. You won't be able to stop yourself. Here goes … Okay, so there was this elephant and this mouse walking along the street one day and …'

Selby went on and on telling his killer joke to Sylvia. Finally he got to the punchline.

'Then, with a twinkle in his eye the elephant said to the mouse …' Selby stopped and looked at Sylvia. 'Are you ready for this?' he asked.

'Yes, of course. Keep going,' a voice said.

Selby looked down at Sylvia in amazement, but before he could say anything, a voice behind him said, 'Well, go ahead!'

Selby spun around to see the two women standing in the doorway.

🐾 Paw note: See 'Selby Smitten' in the book Selby Snaps!.

S

'I don't believe it!' Fiona cried. 'A real, live talking animal!'

'I don't believe it either!' Davina cried. 'I thought you'd just made it all up about animals talking!'

'I thought I had too!' Fiona said.

'Gulp,' Selby gulped, and he could feel the sweat starting to pour off him. 'I've been caught red-mouthed. They know my secret! Maybe if I tell them the punchline, they'll laugh so hard I'll be able to get away. No, that's no good, because they probably didn't hear the joke from the beginning. Besides, they've seen what I look like now. Bogusville is a small town. They're sure to find me. I guess I'll just have to confess.'

'Come on now, talk!' Fiona Fullstop said, bending down. 'We heard you do it! Come on, Sylvia, talk!'

'Sylvia?' Selby thought.

'Yes, talk, Sylvia!' Davina demanded.

'This cat is a goldmine!' Fiona said, pushing Selby out of the way to get to the cat box. 'I'm going to sell this story for millions and billions of dollars! Hey! Who let that dog in here?! Out of the way, you!'

Selby watched as Fiona Fullstop grabbed the cat box and barged out the side door of the theatre with Davina close behind. In a second they'd sped away.

'It was all a bit of a shemozzle,' Mrs Trifle said to Dr Trifle when she got home. 'The book launch was cancelled. By the time I got there the author had run off, taking her cat with her.'

'She probably just didn't want to be embarrassed when her cat didn't talk,' Dr Trifle said. 'Everyone knows that animals can't talk.'

'I don't know,' Mrs Trifle said, giving Selby a good scratch under the chin. 'Sometimes I get the feeling that Selby understands every word we say. Isn't that true, Selby?'

'I could answer that,' Selby thought, sighing secretly at the thoughts of the wonderful times he'd hoped to have with Sylvia, 'but I won't — not yet, anyway.'

YOU LUCKY DOG, YOU!

'What's this game on TV with the balls and the numbers?' Dr Trifle asked as he watched a red ball with a number on it roll down a tube.

'It's called a lottery, dear,' Mrs Trifle said.

'A lottery? Do people win money or something?'

'Yes. They buy a ticket with numbers on it. If their numbers come up they can win millions of dollars.'

Dr Trifle scratched his head, then said, 'What do they do with the money?'

'I guess they buy houses and yachts and they travel.'

'It all sounds pretty silly to me.'

'I agree,' said Mrs Trifle. 'But some people enjoy just the betting part. They feel good when they think they can win and they feel bad when they lose. And if they do win then they jump up and down and scream. They like it when their feelings go up and down like a roller-coaster.'

'Well, I don't,' Dr Trifle said. 'I feel good just the way I am.'

'Oh, how I'd love to win millions of dollars,' Selby thought as he lay nearby. 'But what would I do with the money? I don't really *need* anything. I have something that no amount of money can buy. I've got the wonderful Trifles to look after me.'

Selby watched another ball roll down and stop.

'But wait,' he thought. '*I've* got everything I need, but how about all the poor people who haven't? If I won millions of dollars, I think I'd give it away. That would make me feel really good. What am I thinking? I can't buy a lottery ticket anyway.'

Selby was right. He couldn't buy a lottery ticket. But that didn't mean he couldn't find one — which is exactly what happened . . .

★ ★ ★

Two days later, Selby was out for his morning walk. He'd just passed the Bogusville Newsagency, and there it was on the ground.

'A lottery ticket,' he thought. 'Someone must have dropped it. And they didn't write their name on it so I can't give it back. Hey, this is going to be fun!'

That evening the Trifles went out and Selby lay in front of the TV watching the coloured balls roll down.

'Okay,' Selby thought, 'I want the first one to be seventeen, because that's the first number on my card.'

Selby was daydreaming about giving away millions of dollars, so he wasn't paying attention when the first ball came to a stop. Then he looked and looked again.

'Hey!' he said. 'It *is* seventeen! How do you like that?'

Another ball rolled down. This time Selby was paying attention.

'I need five more,' he thought. 'Wouldn't it be nice if I got my next one? Come on, sixty-three.'

The second ball rolled and rolled and then finally came to a stop.

'Sixty-three!' Selby said. 'Beginner's luck. I got my first two numbers. Maybe I should turn off the TV while I'm still feeling good. I know I won't get three numbers in a row.'

Selby was about to turn off the TV when the next ball dropped.

'Forty-two?' he said, looking at his card. 'That's my third number! I can't believe it! That's three. All I need is three more.'

Selby watched the next ball start rolling down the long slide.

'Eighty-nine,' he thought. 'I want it to be eighty-nine.'

The ball finally stopped.

'Eighty-nine!' Selby cried. 'All I need is two more numbers and I'll be a multi-multi-millionaire! I'll be rich! Oh, please let the next one be seventy-one. Please, please, please!'

Selby took a deep breath.

'Calm down. Lots of people get the first four numbers — it doesn't mean a thing. I've got to stay cool or I'm going to feel really, really horrible when I lose. Come on, number seventy-one. Selby needs a seventy-one.'

The yellow ball rolled down and down the slide. Selby took a deep breath and put his paws over his eyes. Then he opened them very slowly.

'Seventy-one!' he screamed. 'I can't believe it! All I need is a fifteen and I'll win! Come on, fifteen!'

The next ball shot up the tube and then started rolling down and down like the others.

'I think I see a one on it!' Selby squealed while the ball was still rolling. 'Yes, it's definitely a one — and a *five*! There's a one and a five! Oh, please, please don't let it be fifty-one! Come on, fifteen! Come to Selby! Selby wants you! Selby *needs* you! Selby loves you, number fifteen!'

Selby jumped higher and higher till his head almost hit the ceiling. His heart pounded. His lungs were bursting. Sweat poured down his face.

Then finally the ball stopped.

Selby lay on the floor, gasping for breath, as he struggled to make sense of what had happened.

'No,' he mumbled as he crawled towards the TV. 'It's got to be a mistake. Am I wrong? Am I reading the number wrong? No! It's fifteen! It's beautiful, gorgeous number fifteen! *I've won!!!!! Yiiiiippppppppeeeee!*'

Selby panted, clutching his crumpled lottery ticket.

'Some very lucky person,' the announcer on TV said, 'has just won ten million dollars, you lucky dog, you!'

'Little does he know,' Selby thought, 'that the lucky dog *is* a lucky dog. I'm a millionaire! I'm a *ten* millionaire! Oh boy, oh boy, oh boy! What am I going to do with all that dough?'

Visions of things to buy danced in Selby's head.

'Of course, I'll give most of the moolah to charity,' Selby said, 'but I might keep a little bit for a new TV — one of those big flat ones that's as big as a wall. The Trifles wouldn't know where it came from.'

Selby smiled as he imagined the surprise on the Trifles' faces.

'Of course, we'll need one of those new satellite dishes that gets thousands of programs.

And a better DVD player and some of those fantastic huge speakers. We could have a whole entertainment room with seats like a movie theatre. But hang on a tick — this house is too small.'

Selby thought again.

'I'll buy a new house — a nice big one like Madame Mascara's. I'll still have half the money to give to the poor people.'

Selby began to imagine his new life in Trifle Mansion.

'We'll need lots of servants to do the cleaning. It wouldn't be fair if Dr and Mrs Trifle had to do it all. And I'll get them a nice big limo — and a chauffeur to drive it. Maybe I'll only give a quarter of the money away. The poor people should be happy with that,' Selby thought. 'I guess I'd better get down to the newsagency. How will I do this? I think it's suit time.'

Selby dashed under the house and started to put on the dog suit disguise he kept hidden there.

'Once we're in the mansion,' he thought, 'I think I'll tell the Trifles my secret. But if they know I can talk they might put me to work around the house. But hang on, we'll have lots of servants to do the work, so I really can tell them. Hey, and we can travel. I love to travel! So do the Trifles. We'll go everywhere first class. No, forget first class — I'll buy a private jet. And I'll need bodyguards, cos everyone will know I'm a talking dog and that. Okay, so there will only be a teeny bit of money left for the poor people. That's okay. They won't miss it if they never had it. But wait — I guess I should build a private landing strip next to the mansion, so we won't have to go all the way to the airport.'

It was a strange and lumpy figure who walked up to the counter in the newsagency.

'I think I've won today's big jackpot,' it said.

The newsagent stared for a moment.

'You're a dog, right?'

'That's right.'

'Very clever! Now no one's going to know who won, so you can't be hassled for money all the time.'

'That's right.'

'They can't rob you either.'

'Right again.'

'Oh, this is exciting,' the newsagent said. 'I've never sold a winning ticket before. Let me just put your ticket through the machine and make sure that it is the winning ticket.'

The door behind Selby opened slowly and an old man came in, leaning heavily on his walking stick.

'Could you check my ticket to see if I won?' he asked.

'This gentleman here thinks he's won,' the newsagent said.

The man looked at Selby.

'He doesn't look like a gentleman. He looks like a dog,' said the old man, searching his pockets. 'Now, where is my ticket ... I bought it here yesterday. It should be here somewhere, unless I dropped it on the street. Never mind, I'm sure I didn't win anything. I never do. Sorry to trouble you.'

Selby watched the old man shuffling slowly towards the door. He looked at his shabby coat and worn-out shoes.

'It must be his ticket I found,' Selby thought. 'Now I feel awful. Here I was all excited about winning the money and giving it away to the poor — well, maybe a bit of it — and it was a poor little old man who really won it. I can't do this. If I take the money I'll feel guilty forever.'

Selby dashed ahead, opening the door for the man and quickly slipping the ticket into his pocket.

'Excuse me,' Selby said, 'why don't you look through your pockets again?'

'Oh, no, Mr Dog,' the old man answered. 'The man said that you won it anyway.'

'Well, maybe I didn't. I'm not very good with numbers. I might have read them wrong. Have another look . . . please?'

'It doesn't matter,' the old man said. 'What would I do with all that money anyway?'

'For starters, you could buy some new clothes,' Selby thought. (He didn't say it, he only thought it.) Then he said, 'Please, let me have a look.'

Selby pulled open the pocket where he'd put the ticket.

'It's there,' he said. 'Look!'

'Goodness me. So it is.'

Selby took the ticket to the counter.

The newsagent put the ticket into the lottery machine. Suddenly bells rang and whistles whistled and buzzers buzzed.

'You won, Mr Penticost!' the newsagent cried. 'Sorry, mate,' he said to Selby. 'I guess you lose. And all that trouble with the dog suit, too.'

'But I feel good and that's all that matters,' Selby thought on his way home. 'I had all the fun of winning the money and then the double fun of giving it to someone who really needed it. What could be better?'

That evening on TV the Trifles saw the shouting and cheering crowd at the newsagency.

'Can you believe this?' Mrs Trifle said. 'Someone here in Bogusville just won ten million dollars in the lottery! It's Mr Penticost.'

'Maybe he can buy himself some new clothes,' Dr Trifle said. 'And fix up that broken-down house.'

'He won't, you know,' Mrs Trifle said. 'That man is the biggest cheapskate in the world. He's already inherited millions of dollars and he's never spent a cent of it.'

'And what will you do with the money?' the lottery man asked Mr Penticost. 'Buy a mansion? A yacht? An aeroplane? Or are you going to give it to charity?'

'Charity?!' the old man said. 'You've got to be joking! I'll save it. And then it'll all go to Wilbur when I'm gone.'

'Who's Wilbur?'

'My cockatoo. Did you know that cockatoos can live to be eighty years old? With all this money, I know he'll always have enough birdseed.'

'Oh, groan,' Selby thought. 'I could have had all the money! I could have given it to charity! How much birdseed can Wilbur possibly eat?!'

'The funny thing,' the old man said, 'is that I was in a bit of a shemozzle — I couldn't find my ticket. So a very kind dog looked in one of my pockets and found it.'

'A dog did that?'

'Yes, and later on I looked in another pocket and found another ticket for the same lottery. I must have bought two tickets without knowing it.'

'Groan and double groan,' Selby thought. 'The lost ticket wasn't even his after all! Life just isn't fair.'

'Hi, guys, have you heard the exciting news?' Aunt Jetty said as she bounded through the doorway. 'That old cheapskate, Mr Penticost, just won ten million bucks! *Ten million smackeroos!* Why do the wrong people always win? I never win anything.'

'Neither do we,' Mrs Trifle said, 'but then, we don't buy the tickets in the first place.'

'Well, I do,' Aunt Jetty said. 'In fact, I bought one for today's lottery but I lost it. I think I must have dropped it when I left the newsagency this morning.'

'I just changed my mind,' Selby thought, as he struggled to keep from smiling. 'Maybe life is fair after all — well, a little bit.'

THE BLOOD OF THE WOLFMAN

Hi, this is Selby and I'm going to tell this story myself. It's too complicated to let Duncan tell it. Besides, he might try to make it funny. One thing it definitely is *not* is funny. Anyway, I'm going to tell it myself, if that's okay with you.

It was Saturday evening. Dr Trifle was on a stepladder twisting a little metal thingy into the ceiling. What was I doing? I was just lying there sort of watching.

Dr Trifle said, 'If this new invention of mine works, everyone will want one.'

Which is what he always says about his new inventions.

So Mrs Trifle said, 'That's what you always say about your new inventions.'

'Do I?' he asked. (Dr Trifle always forgets things.)

'Yes. You even said it about the hair restorer you invented this morning.'

'The what?' (See what I mean about Dr Trifle forgetting?)

That morning he'd invented some stuff to make hair grow back if you're bald. At least, that's what he hoped it would do. He'd put it in an empty bottle of Beautifying and Anti-Ageing Cream.

'This,' Mrs Trifle said, picking up the bottle. 'You said that everyone would want it, but I don't think so. The bald patch on your head is still just as bald as it was.'

'Is it?' Dr Trifle said, tipping his head so he could see the top of it in the mirror. 'Oh, well, throw it away. But this invention will be a winner.'

Mrs Trifle looked up.

'It looks like a water sprinkler, like the ones you see in offices.'

'That's exactly what it is. But those ones only start spraying water when things really get burning. The heat turns them on. My VAPO invention is much better.'

'VAPO?'

'Voice-Activated Putter-Outer. The second you see the tiniest spark or a bit of smoke, you just yell you-know-what and *whoooooooooosh*! water sprays everywhere.'

'What is it that you have to yell?' Mrs Trifle said.

'You-know-what.'

'So if I yelled out "you-know-what" right now it would start sprinkling?'

'No, you don't actually yell "you-know-what". You have to yell …' Dr Trifle scrambled down from the ladder and whispered in Mrs Trifle's ear.

'Oh,' she said. 'So you have to yell "Fire".'

'Shhhh! Not so loud, you'll set it off,' Dr Trifle said. 'Now, isn't that the best you-know-what putter-outer invention ever?'

'Maybe, but what if a … a you-know-what starts and there's no one around to yell … you-know-what?'

'Hmmm,' Dr Trifle hmmmed. 'I hadn't thought of that. Oh well.'

'Goodness me, look at the time!' said Mrs Trifle. 'Jetty will be here any minute. She's leaving her boys with us tonight while she does her Aggressiveness Training class.'

Now, as anyone who's read any of the stories about me knows, Aunt Jetty hates me. I think she really started to hate me when I bit her on the bum. But that's a different story. ❧ Why she thinks she needs aggressiveness training is beyond me. She's already as aggressive as a crocodile with two heads.

Anyway, her dreadful sons, Willy and Billy, have always hated me. So when the brats come over, I usually disappear. Only this time Mrs Trifle had put a big lacy tablecloth over the dining-room table, so I just crawled under it and hid.

Minutes later, Willy and Billy were running around the house. Willy was shooting arrows at Billy and Billy was hitting Willy with his cricket bat.

'Settle down, boys, before you kill each other,' Mrs Trifle ordered.

❧ *Paw note: See 'Selby Bites Back' in the book* Selby Supersnoop.   S

'It's okay, Sis,' Aunt Jetty said. 'The arrows have rubber tips and the cricket bat is only plastic. They can't hurt each other.'

'I'm not just worried about them,' Mrs Trifle said. 'They're knocking things over everywhere. Something's going to get broken.'

'Time out!' Aunt Jetty roared, putting her hands up to make a T shape. 'Stop it right now!'

Now, when Aunt Jetty roars, she really roars! Willy and Billy stopped in their tracks.

'But we're not hurtin' nuffin',' Willy said.

'Well, it's time to stop,' Mrs Trifle said. 'We have some books you boys can read.'

'Books?! Yuck! We want to watch our DVDs,' said Billy.

'What are they?' Mrs Trifle asked.

Willy got a DVD out of his bag and I could see a horrified look on Mrs Trifle's face.

'Oh no, you don't,' she said. 'You're not going to watch a film called *The Blood of the Wolfman*. Look what it says on the back: "Lock your doors and windows! Hairy Harry the head-chopping monster from hell is back."'

'Wolfman?!' Aunt Jetty said, snatching the

DVD from Willy. 'You boys said it was a nature film.'

'It's not scary, Mummy,' Willy said. 'It's just funny when he chops heads off and that.'

'You're not watching it!'

'Is this one okay, Mummy?' Willy asked, handing another DVD to Aunt Jetty.

'*Krazy Kitties Go on Holidays*,' she read. '"Another fun-filled frolic, when Karen and Karla Kitty get lost in a fun fair." Yes, you can watch this one.'

'Okay, Mummy,' Willy and Billy said together.

'*The Blood of the Wolfman*,' Aunt Jetty said to her sister. 'Can you believe the things kids watch today? When we were kids our parents read us stories like *Goldilocks and the Three Bears*. They were scary enough! I used to be terrified when the three bears blew the house down.'

'I think that was *The Three Little Pigs*,' said Mrs Trifle. 'What scared me was the wolf in *Little Red Riding Hood*.'

'Yes, I remember,' Aunt Jetty laughed. 'When Mum said, "What big teeth you have, Grandma", you'd put your hands over your eyes and scream, "It's a wolf! It's a wolf!"'

Dr Trifle laughed.

'When the giant in *Jack and the Beanstalk* said, "Fee fi fo fum",' Dr Trifle said, 'I used to scream, "Look out! Here he comes!"'

Dr and Mrs Trifle and Aunt Jetty all had a big laugh.

'Uh-oh! I'm going to be late for my Aggressiveness Training class,' Aunt Jetty said, leaping up and giving a sideways kick. '*Hiiii-yah!*'

Now this is the bit that I saw but I don't think anyone else did. Just as she got to the door, Aunt Jetty noticed the bottle of Dr Trifle's hair restorer in the rubbish.

'What have we here? Beautifying and Anti-Ageing Cream,' she mumbled as she slipped it into her sports bag.

Anyway, later when Dr Trifle was back in his workroom and Mrs Trifle was in the study, Willy said, 'Hey, Billy! Let's watch the *Krazy Kitties*.'

'Yeah, right,' Billy said. 'He he he.'

I could tell from the giggling that they were up to no good. Sure enough, out of the *Krazy Kitties Go on Holidays* DVD case came *The Blood of the Wolfman*. Those sneaky brats had switched the DVDs!

Anyway, they started watching it — and it was awful! It was about this werewolf called Hairy Harry who went around killing people. The only way to kill him was to put a piece of wood through his heart. Anyway, somebody did kill him in the end. *Sooooooo* gross!

'If he came in here I could kill him with my cricket bat!' Billy said.

'No, you couldn't,' Willy said. 'He'd chop your head off.'

'He couldn't because I'd get him first.'

'No, you wouldn't, Billy. I'd shoot him in the heart with my bow and arrow and he'd be dead.'

'Ha ha. He'd chop your head off cos your arrows are only rubber.'

'Oh yeah? Well then I'd pull the rubber bit off and shoot him through the heart and he'd be really, really dead, stupid.'

That's when Mrs Trifle came out of the study.

'How was the movie?' she asked the boys.

'It was good,' they both said.

'Well, your mother just rang to say she's going to be late. So you can sleep on the lounge till she gets back.'

Mrs Trifle put a blanket over the boys and turned off the lights. Then she and Dr Trifle went to bed.

So there I was, wide awake and totally spooked by the stupid movie. Every time I heard a noise I thought it was Hairy Harry coming to chop my head off. Of course, Willy and Billy went right to sleep.

Anyway, about an hour later I heard the front door slowly creaking open. At first I thought, 'It's the werewolf!' but then I thought, 'Get a grip, Selby, it's only Aunt Jetty.'

I looked out from under the tablecloth and there was this really hairy hand coming around the door.

'Gulp,' I thought. 'It's him! But it can't be!'

The hairy hand was followed by another hairy hand, and then a hairy head. There, creeping into the lounge room, was Hairy Harry!

Now, I don't know what you'd do if a hairy head-chopping monster came into your lounge room. I don't reckon you'd think it over or anything. I mean, you probably wouldn't say to yourself, 'A hairy head-chopping monster just came into my lounge room. What should I do about it? Let me think this over.' No, I reckon you'd scream. And that's just what I did. I yelled out in plain English, 'Help! He's here! The monster's here! Run for your lives!'

The surprising thing was that the monster screamed too.

'A monster! A monster!' it screamed.

That's when I realised that the hairy head-chopping werewolf was really Aunt Jetty! And all the hair was from Dr Trifle's hair restorer, because she'd thought it was Beautifying and Anti-Ageing Cream and put it all over herself!

Anyway, Aunt Jetty ran down the hallway to get away from the monster and she suddenly saw herself in the hall mirror. Of course, she didn't know she was covered in hair, and in the darkness she didn't know that the hairy monster running towards her was herself.

Suddenly she leapt into the air with a '*Hiiii-yah!*', kicking the mirror and smashing it to bits.

'Where'd you go, you devil?' she screamed, and she raced back, kicking in every direction. '*Hiiii-yah! Hiiii-yah! Hiiii-yah!*'

Now at this point the boys woke up and started screaming at the top of their lungs, 'Help! It's him! It's him! Help!' while running around trying to keep out of the way of their kicking mother.

Hearing all the noise, Mrs Trifle tore out of the bedroom and when she saw the hairy, kicking monster she suddenly must have gone back to being a little girl again, because she put her hands over her eyes and screamed, 'It's a wolf! It's a wolf!'

The thing about Dr Trifle is that he's a very sound sleeper. Almost nothing wakes him up. But he's not a sound enough sleeper to sleep through four people screaming at the top of their lungs, and one of them kicking the furniture to bits. So, still dazed from his deep sleep, Dr Trifle stepped into the hallway, rubbing his face with his hands.

It was then that he must have felt the patch of new hair growing on the top of his head where he used to be bald. And it was then that he saw the dark hairy figure kicking and roaring like a gorilla fighting off a herd of attacking hyenas.

It was suddenly all too much for him and he, too, sank back into his *Jack and the Beanstalk* days.

'Look out!' he screamed. 'Here he comes! Look out! Look out!'

Billy was running around bashing his mother with his plastic cricket bat until she kicked him across the room.

Willy, meanwhile, ripped the rubber tips off his wooden arrows, took aim at his mother and drew the bow back so far I thought it would break.

'*Shoot him in the heart, Willy!*' Billy screamed. '*Shoot the werewolf! Ready! Aim! ...*'

When I saw Willy about to shoot his mother through the heart, I knew I had to do something.

I leapt out from under the table and was about to yell out in plain English, 'Stop this! Stop it right now! It's not a hairy head-chopping monster, it's only Aunt Jetty!' when suddenly Billy yelled, '*Fire!*' and Willy let the arrow go.

The arrow flew through the air as fast as a bullet, heading straight for Aunt Jetty. For a minute I thought of jumping into the air and letting it hit me instead, but then I thought better of it.

Suddenly there was water everywhere. Billy yelling '*Fire!*' had set off Dr Trifle's fire putter-outer invention.

Aunt Jetty had gone into a fighting crouch, kicking this way and that with her bottom pointing in my direction. I knew there was only one thing to do to save her. I sprang towards her, flying through the air like an eagle after a rat.

And that's when I bit Aunt Jetty on the bum — again. Only this time it was on purpose.

'*Yooooouuuuuuch!*' Aunt Jetty screamed, straightening up — as you would do if you were bent over and someone bit you on the bum — and the arrow whizzed past, just missing her.

Suddenly the wet tuft of hair on Dr Trifle's head slid off and hit the floor. And then all the hair from the hairy monster fell off too.

'Jetty!' Mrs Trifle cried. 'It's you!'

Anyway, so that's what happened. Later the Trifles and Aunt Jetty laughed when they talked

about 'The Big Shemozzle'. Aunt Jetty blamed it all on the boys watching a DVD they shouldn't have. Mrs Trifle blamed Dr Trifle for inventing his hair restorer. Dr Trifle blamed Mrs Trifle for screaming so much and waking him up. Willy blamed Billy for hitting his mother with his cricket bat. And everyone blamed Willy for almost killing Aunt Jetty.

I was the only one who didn't get any blame, and really, when you think about it, it was my fault. It never would have happened if I hadn't screamed when Aunt Jetty came in the door.

The surprising thing was that Aunt Jetty was actually happy that I bit her on the bum.

'You saved my life, you smelly old thing,' she said. 'If you hadn't nipped me, I'd have been killed.'

And that's when the most horrible thing of all happened — Aunt Jetty kissed me.

Yucko!

SEEING-EYE SELBY

'You'll like my old friend, Bertha,' Cousin Wilhemina said to Mrs Trifle. 'She's just visiting for the weekend. You wouldn't mind putting her up, would you?'

'No, I'd be happy to,' said Mrs Trifle.

'She's a big woman,' Cousin Wilhemina said. 'Likes her food. But she's not fussy. She'll eat anything. And so will Fred.'

'Fred? Who's Fred, her husband?'

Wilhemina laughed.

'Oh no, she isn't married. Fred isn't a *who*, he's a *what*. He's not a person, he's a *thing*.'

'You want me to put up a strange woman and ... and a thing?'

'He's a dog,' Wilhemina said. 'Fred is Bertha's dog.'

'Now hang on,' Selby thought. 'I'm a dog and I'm not just a *thing*. What is she on about?'

'You didn't mention that your friend is bringing her dog,' Mrs Trifle said. 'What if he doesn't get along with Selby? Oh, well, I guess we could leave him outdoors.'

'No, you can't do that. Fred is Bertha's seeing-eye dog.'

'Her what?'

'Her seeing-eye dog. Her *guide* dog. He leads her everywhere and sleeps by her bed. You can't separate them.'

'Oh, I get it,' Mrs Trifle said, 'your friend is blind. Why didn't you say so? I'm sure she and her dog won't be any trouble at all. Now I remember Bertha. You two used to go hiking together, didn't you?'

'Many years ago,' Cousin Wilhemina said. 'She became a very serious mountaineer. She lost her sight when she came down with mountain madness on the tallest mountain in the world and then fell off a cliff.'

'Mount Everest, was it?' Mrs Trifle said.

'No, that's not the tallest anymore. Not since they discovered Mount Selby in Antarctica.'

'Mount Selby,' Selby thought. 'My mountain. I love that mountain — even if it did almost kill me.' 🐾

'So when will your friend be coming over?' Mrs Trifle asked.

'She's here. She's in the car right now. I'll bring her in.'

Selby watched as the big woman and her enormous dog came through the door. Fred stared at Selby and silently curled his lip, showing a full set of pointy teeth.

'Good grief,' Selby thought as he backed away. 'This is no dog — it's a shark! Settle down, big fella. I won't hurt you.'

That afternoon, Mrs Trifle and Bertha had lunch while Fred ate all of Selby's Dry-Mouth Dog Biscuits.

'Blindness isn't much fun,' Bertha told Mrs Trifle, 'but my life is pretty normal, thanks to

🐾 Paw note: See the story 'Selby Snowbound' in the book Selby Snowbound.   S

Fred. He gets me around fairly well. I do sometimes miss getting out into nature — hiking, mountain climbing, kayaking — the sort of things I used to do before my accident. But never mind about me, you've got work to do.'

'I am a little busy,' Mrs Trifle said. 'I have a bit of work to do for my council meeting.'

'Well, I might just go for a walk,' Bertha said. 'Oh, I forgot — sore leg.'

'I'm terribly sorry,' Mrs Trifle said. 'I hope you feel better soon.'

'It's not me,' the woman said, 'it's Fred. I must have walked him too hard yesterday.'

'I'll take you for a walk,' Mrs Trifle said. 'My work can wait.'

'I couldn't ask you to do that. You're a busy woman. I have some books on CD that I can listen to. But wait a minute — what about that dog of yours?'

'What about him?'

'Maybe he could walk me around the block.'

'I suppose so, but he's not a guide dog. Guide dogs have to be very well trained, don't they?'

'What's so hard about being a guide dog?' Selby thought. 'I could take her for a walk.'

'Yes, they have to be well trained,' Bertha said. 'They can't just go chasing cars or cats or sticks —'

'I don't chase cars or cats or sticks,' Selby thought. 'The only thing I ever chased was a peanut prawn that was falling off a plate — and I caught it before it hit the ground.'

'— and they have to be responsible —'

'I'm responsible.'

'— and, most of all, they have to be intelligent.'

'Hey, hang on, I'm intelligent. I'd be a terrific guide dog. I can even read signs. What guide dog can do that? And I could ask for directions (but I wouldn't, of course).'

'I'll tell you what,' Bertha said, 'put a leash on your dog. I'll take my white stick, and I'm sure between the two of us I'll be able to go for a short walk.'

'Are you sure?'

'Yes, of course I'm sure and I insist.'

'I'll show her,' Selby thought.

It was a careful, responsible and intelligent dog that led the blind woman up the driveway to the street and then along the footpath.

'Come on, dog, let's get a wriggle on,' the woman said. 'How am I going to get any exercise at this speed?'

Selby led the woman twice around the block and then once around again.

'You're going fine, dog,' the woman said. 'Another hour should do it.'

'Another hour? No wonder Fred is lame. And I'm beginning to feel like a merry-go-round horse going round and round and round,' Selby thought. 'I think I'll take her somewhere a bit more interesting. How about a walk along the creek?'

Selby stopped and looked both ways before crossing the street.

'Hey, we've crossed a street,' the woman said. 'Good one, dog. Take me somewhere interesting.'

Selby led the woman down the street and then across a field and up a hill.

'Bravo!' she said. 'Come on, dog, my leg muscles are just starting to work! Keep it up.'

'She's loving it,' Selby thought. 'I'll bet Fred never gives her a workout like this. He's too careful. She needs an uncareful, responsible, intelligent dog like me.'

As the hill got steeper and steeper, Selby dug his paws into the dirt and scrambled up and up. Around boulders and bushes they went. Selby kept his face towards the ground making sure there was nothing to trip on. Suddenly . . .

Clonk!

'Ooooooh,' Bertha groaned.

Selby turned quickly to see the big woman sitting on the ground.

'Oh, no!' he thought. 'A low branch! She clonked her head because I was looking at the ground. This guide dog stuff is trickier than I thought.'

'A branch,' Bertha said, reaching out and patting Selby and then getting slowly to her feet. 'I haven't clonked my head like that since I went walking in a jungle in Africa. What a trip that was. Brings back old memories. Come on, dog, what are we waiting for?'

Selby kept going up the hill, but this time he watched for low branches while Bertha lifted her stick in the air to do the same.

'This is fun,' Selby thought. 'I'll bet she hasn't had a walk like this since her mountaineering days.'

On and on, up and up Selby raced with the woman until . . .

'Ooooo, uuuuh, woooooo!'

Selby turned around to find the woman on the ground again.

'Uh-oh,' he thought. 'Where did that rabbit hole come from? Just when I start to look up for branches there are things to look down for, like rabbit holes.'

Bertha struggled to her feet.

'A hole,' she said. 'That reminds me of the time I fell down a crack in a glacier in South America. Well, leg's not broken. Everything's still working. Come on, dog, let's get a move on while there's still time in the day. Oh, how I love being out in nature again! This is wonderful!'

Selby trudged on, and then started down the other side of the hill.

Suddenly he saw something.

'The sun,' he thought. 'It's not there anymore. It must have set. If we don't get back soon, we're going to be stuck out here after dark.'

Selby looked around at the trees and fields below.

'We should go back the way we came, but it's too late,' he thought. 'We'll have to take a short-cut.'

Down and down they went till they got to the banks of Bogusville Creek.

'Oh, no,' Selby thought, 'we're on the wrong side of the creek and the bridge is washed out! The only way across is over the fallen log. I can't possibly get her over that. But we have to. It's getting cold and we'll freeze if we don't get home.'

'What's that? Water?' Bertha said. 'Do I hear rushing water? What a wonderful sound. That reminds me of the time I'd been walking for a week along the Oronoco River and I knew I had to get across it or starve to death. And the only way across was over a slippery log.'

'Well, that's exactly what we have here,' Selby thought (he didn't say it, though, he only thought it).

Selby walked towards the log and then started across it.

'I can't believe I'm doing this!' he screamed in his brain. 'And I'm not only doing it but I'm pulling a blind woman with me!'

Selby and Bertha were about halfway across when the rushing water suddenly moved the log, sending Selby plunging one way into the creek and Bertha the other.

'I'm going to drown!' Selby thought. 'I've got to get back on the log.'

Selby scrambled up onto the log again as he watched Bertha thrashing around in the swirling water.

'I have to speak now or she'll drown!' he thought. And then he said out loud, 'Hey, lady! Stop struggling and I'll pull you.'

'What was that?' Bertha spluttered.

'Don't let go of the leash!' Selby cried. 'Hang on tight! Can you do that?'

'Yes, I think I can!' she yelled back.

Selby crept across the log, pulling the woman alongside till she finally crawled ashore on the muddy bank.

'You're going to be okay,' Selby said. 'Just rest for a minute and everything's going to be all right.'

It was a tired and wet dog that finally made his way home, leading a big woman behind him.

'This is it,' Selby thought. 'Now she knows my secret and everyone's going to find out. Oh, well, it's my own fault. I never should have tried to be a guide dog.'

'Bertha!' Mrs Trifle cried. 'What happened? You're all muddy and wet! Your clothes are all torn! What did Selby do to you?'

'I don't know,' the woman said, heaving a sigh. 'To be honest it was quite a shemozzle. He was hopeless. He almost killed me.'

'I did,' Selby thought. 'I guess I did. And now she's going to reveal my secret. Maybe I should say something first.'

Selby was just about to say, 'Okay, so I'm a hopeless guide dog and I'm sorry about that but at least I saved her life', when suddenly Bertha spoke.

'Of course, it was all my fault,' the woman said. 'Fortunately a very kind man helped me to safety and, to tell the truth, I had the best adventure I've had for years!'

'And so did I,' Selby thought, sighing with relief that his secret was still safe. 'So did I.'

DRY-MOUTH DRAMA

'Stop! Don't eat that!' Mrs Trifle said as she took a biscuit out of Dr Trifle's hand.

'What's wrong?' Dr Trifle asked. 'It's just a Heavenly Munch Suga-Kreem Caramel Biscuit.'

'And it's the very worst thing you could eat!'

'But I love Heavenly Munch Biscuits. They taste great. You make it sound like they've been poisoned.'

'They might as well have been. Do you know how much fat is in them?'

Dr Trifle looked at the packet.

'It says "Fifty per cent fat-free",' he said. 'That means that only half of them have fat in them and the other half don't. I'll just pick out the fat-free ones and throw the other ones away. Now, how can I tell which is which?'

'It doesn't mean that at all. Fifty per cent fat-free means that half of each and every biscuit is fat. And that's really bad for you.'

'But they're yummy.'

'Well, you're not having any!' Mrs Trifle threw the packet in the rubbish and took something from the cupboard. 'You can have one of these Nature-Good Ultra-Thin No-Fat Dry Rice Wafers — but only one.'

'But those things are terrible. They disappear when they touch your tongue. And they taste like sawdust.'

'They're good for you. Eat one and then let's go for a good, long power walk to burn off the calories.'

'Dr Trifle has nothing to complain about,' Selby thought after the Trifles had gone out. 'They're just lucky they don't have to eat what they feed me. Those Dry-Mouth Dog Biscuits are disgusting!'

Selby looked at the label on a new packet of Dry-Mouth Dog Biscuits.

'"Ten per cent sawdust-free." I guess that's not too bad,' Selby thought. 'Now hang on a tick! Ten per cent sawdust-*free* means that it's *ninety per cent* sawdust! I might as well eat a log! What am I, a termite? I'm sure they never used to have this much sawdust in them.'

Selby grabbed the old packet of Dry-Mouth Dog Biscuits.

'Just as I thought! This packet says that it's *twenty per cent* sawdust-free. That's only eighty per cent sawdust. They keep putting more and more sawdust in them. What kind of people would do a thing like that?'

Suddenly a light went on in Selby's head.

'Hey!' he thought. 'It says that Dry-Mouth Dog Biscuits are made by DMDB Enterprises over in Poshfield. I think I'll just nip over there for a look.'

On the edge of Poshfield, Selby found a big building with a sign that said:

DMDB Enterprises
The home of Dry-Mouth Dog Biscuits

Then there was a picture of a smiling dog and, under it, the words:

If he could talk, he'd ask for Dry-Mouth Dog Biscuits.

'I can talk,' Selby thought, 'and there's no way I'd ask for them.'

Selby peered in through a filthy window. Inside the building, a huge machine cranked out rows and rows of dog biscuits and put them into packets. Selby opened a steel door and crept inside. The floor was covered in grease and water, and the air was filled with smoke and steam.

'This is weird,' Selby thought as he looked up at the tanks and tubes and conveyor belts that crisscrossed the building. 'There are no people here. It's all automatic.'

Selby took a dog biscuit from the conveyor belt, nibbled a corner off it, and then spat it on the floor.

'Yuck!' he cried. 'These are worse than before! No wonder. The packets now say *five* per cent sawdust-free! Ninety-five per cent is sawdust!'

Suddenly Selby heard voices arguing behind him.

'Bartleby Boffin!' one of them boomed. 'I own this company and you'll do as I say!'

'But — but Mr Dorset,' the other man said, 'we can't put any more sawdust in them. They're ninety-five per cent sawdust already.'

'It's Denis Dorset!' Selby thought. 'The mayor of Poshfield! So he's the guy who owns Dry-Mouth Dog Biscuits. I might have known.'

'We have to cut costs,' Denis said. 'I'm not making enough money. Sawdust is really really cheap, Bart. Put more in. Make the biscuits ninety-nine per cent sawdust.'

'But Mr Dorset, we can't possibly write that they're only one per cent sawdust-free on the label. Dogs will hate them.'

'You're missing the whole point, you lunkhead,' Denis Dorset said. '*Dogs* don't buy dog biscuits. *People* buy dog biscuits. And dogs can't talk, so they can't tell their owners how awful the dreadful things taste.'

'Ninety-nine per cent sawdust,' Bartleby said. 'Dog owners will notice.'

'Okay then, don't call it sawdust.'

'But we have to say what's in them.'

'Call it Vitamin S — S for sawdust. Now just do as I say or I'll sack you the way I sacked everyone else.'

'Okay,' Bart said meekly. 'I'll do it tomorrow. It's time to close up for the night.'

'Don't you dare! You stay and keep the machine running. We need to make another ten thousand packets tonight. You can order some takeaway food for yourself if you get hungry.'

Denis Dorset sped off in his long limousine while Bartleby Boffin turned a few knobs and dials and then took a spoonful of dog biscuit mix and ate it.

'Disgusting!' he said. 'Tastes like old socks. Poor dogs — I feel sorry for them. And to think, Dry-Mouth Dog Biscuits are about to taste even worse.'

Suddenly the man noticed Selby.

'Hello, little guy,' he said. 'How did you get in here?'

He leant down and gave Selby a pat.

'I love dogs,' he said. 'And that makes my job even harder.'

Bartleby Boffin scooped up some of the dog

biscuit mix in a spoon and gave it to Selby. Selby licked it and then spat it out.

'Awful, isn't it?' the man said. 'Sorry about that. Follow me, boy, and I'll give you some decent food.'

Selby followed the man into a laboratory. There on the shelves were boxes and boxes of Dry-Mouth Dog Biscuits, each one with a date written on it. He opened one.

'Have one of these,' he said. 'Thirty years old. That's when we used to make excellent dog biscuits — long before Mayor Dorset took over.'

Selby tasted it.

'Not bad,' he thought. 'Not as good as people-food, but not too bad.'

'You're making me hungry, dog,' the man said. 'Now to get some food for myself . . .'

The man picked up the phone and dialled.

'Is that The Spicy Onion? I'd like to order some takeaway food, please.'

'The Spicy Onion,' Selby sighed in his mind. 'I love that place. This guy has good taste in food after all.'

'Yes, I'd like one of those rice dishes with everything in it. Yes, that's the one. That's for me,

Bartleby Boffin at the Dry-Mouth Dog Biscuit Factory in Poshfield. Thanks.'

'Oh no!' Selby thought. 'He doesn't know about their peanut prawns, the most delicious food in the whole world! How can I tell him?'

As soon as the man went out into the factory again, Selby picked up the telephone.

'The Spicy Onion? Bartleby Boffin here,' Selby said, imitating Bart's voice. 'Cancel the rice thingy and bring me an order of peanut prawns, please.'

Within a few minutes the food had been delivered and Bart sat at a bench ready to eat.

'Hmmm, what are these?' he said. 'They smell like prawns cooked in some sort of peanut sauce. They must have brought me the wrong order.'

The man took one bite and then another and another until he was down to the last prawn.

'This is heavenly!' he sighed. 'It has to be the most delicious food in the whole world! Here, boy, the last one's for you.'

Selby gobbled the last prawn, and in a flash the man picked up the phone again.

'The Spicy Onion?' he said. 'It's me again, Bart Boffin at Dry-Mouth. Could you send me another two orders of peanut prawns. No, make that five.'

'Five orders of peanut prawns!' Selby thought. 'Oh goody. I wonder if he'll give me some more.'

'I've just changed my mind,' said Bart.

'Uh-oh,' Selby thought.

'Instead of five orders, bring me one hundred orders. Yes, one hundred. One zero zero. And make it snappy.'

'He's gone completely bonkers!' Selby thought. 'He's been working too hard and eating too much dog food. He can't possibly eat one hundred orders of peanut prawns even if I help him.'

Soon the Spicy Onion van had unloaded the one hundred orders of peanut prawns and driven off. For the next hour, Selby and Bart ate peanut prawns till they were sick of them. But there were still ninety-five containers left.

'I'll bet you're wondering what I'm going to do with these,' the man said to Selby. 'Just watch.'

Bart emptied one after another of the containers of peanut prawns into the dog biscuit mix.

'If you're anything like other dogs,' he said to Selby, 'then dogs are going to love these new biscuits. Who cares if I get the sack? At least I will have made a few dogs happy.'

'What a nice man,' Selby thought as he smelled the heavenly smell of the new peanut prawn-flavoured biscuits coming along the conveyor belt.

Bartleby Boffin picked up a biscuit and broke it in half. He gave half to Selby and ate the other half himself.

'Not as good as real peanut prawns,' Selby thought, 'but still delicious.'

'Delicious,' Bart said, agreeing with Selby without knowing it.

The first hint that something strange was about to happen came with sounds in the distance.

'What's that?' Selby thought as the sounds grew louder and louder. 'I've never heard anything like it before. It sounds like a stampede!'

Sure enough, dogs from all around Poshfield and Bogusville ran towards the wonderful smell that came from the factory. Within a minute a huge pack of dogs had rounded the corner of the building and come in through the open door. They tore by Selby and Bart and started grabbing biscuits and jumping into the vat of Dry-Mouth Dog Biscuit mix.

'This is fantastic!' cried Bart. 'These are going to be the greatest biscuits ever!'

'Have you seen the price of the new Dry-Mouth Dog Biscuits?' Dr Trifle asked Mrs Trifle when he held up a package of New Improved Dry-Mouth Dog Biscuits with Vitamin PP. 'They're twice as expensive as the old ones.'

'Yes, but Selby loves them,' Mrs Trifle said. 'He ate the whole package we bought yesterday.'

'They smell yummy,' Dr Trifle said. 'I could eat them myself.'

'Apparently the Dry-Mouth Dog Biscuit Company is doing huge business in them,' Mrs Trifle said. 'Denis Dorset must be getting very rich.'

'Well, that part of it is too bad,' Selby thought. 'But at least I've made a lot of dogs very happy — including myself.'

'This may sound funny,' Dr Trifle said, 'but they smell a bit like those lovely peanut prawns they make at The Spicy Onion Restaurant.'

'Goodness, I think you're right — but they can't be,' Mrs Trifle said, looking at the label. 'If

they were anything like that there would have to be a warning that there are peanuts in them.'

'Really? What's wrong with peanuts?'

'Nothing, usually. It's just that some people — and that goes for dogs too — are allergic to peanuts. They can even die from eating them, so every food that has peanuts in it has to say so on the label.'

'Uh-oh,' Selby thought. 'What have I done?! Dogs could be dropping dead all over the place because of me! Okay, it's very unlikely, but if even one dog died because of me, I'd hate myself. What a shemozzle! I've got to do something — but what?'

All night long Selby lay awake on his mat thinking of a dog that might be choking on a New Improved Dry-Mouth Dog Biscuit with Vitamin PP. In the morning, after the Trifles had each had a Nature-Good Ultra-Thin No-Fat Dry Rice Wafer and were out for their power walk, Selby ran to the telephone and dialled Denis Dorset.

'Excuse me, Mr Dorset,' Selby said. 'I just wanted to talk to you about something.'

'What can I do for you?'

'It's about your New Improved Dry-Mouth Dog Biscuits with Vitamin PP.'

'Aha! So you'd like to place an order, would you? I'm afraid there's a six-month waiting list. I'm now getting orders from all around the world. We're about to build a bigger factory.'

'Well, don't,' Selby said.

'What do you mean?'

'I happen to know that Vitamin PP stands for peanut prawns. And peanut prawns have peanuts in them, and peanuts can be very dangerous. If you don't stop making them, I'll sue you.'

'You'll *what*? Who are you?'

'None of your business. All you need to know is that I had one of your new dog biscuits and I landed in hospital. I almost choked to death because I'm allergic to peanut prawns. And now I'm going to sue you if you don't stop making them.'

'That happened to you?'

'Yes.'

'But dog biscuits are for dogs,' Denis Dorset said. 'You're not a dog, are you?'

'Yes — I mean, no. I mean, it was actually my dog that was allergic. And he can't sue you

112

— because he's a dog — but I'm going to. And I'm going to tell everyone in the government and they'll close down your factory.'

There was a moment's silence.

'This is blackmail,' Denis Dorset said.

'It certainly is,' Selby agreed. 'And you'd better do as I say.'

One week later it was a very hungry dog who gagged as he chewed a Classic Dry-Mouth Dog Biscuit with even more Vitamin S than before. But he was a happy dog, too.

Selby struggled not to smile as he thought of the dogs with peanut allergies that he'd saved. And he struggled even harder not to smile as he thought about getting Denis Dorset to change the mixture.

Dr Trifle dropped some more biscuits into Selby's bowl.

'These dog biscuits don't smell like the ones Selby finished last week,' he said to Mrs Trifle. 'Remember, those ones smelled like peanuts and prawns?'

'Yes, I do remember,' Mrs Trifle said. 'But all this talk of peanuts and prawns is making me hungry. Why don't you ring The Spicy Onion Restaurant and get an order of those lovely peanut prawns they make?'

'What a good idea,' Dr Trifle said, reaching for the telephone.

'Oh, groan,' Selby thought. 'Now I'm going to have to watch the Trifles eat the very food that I want.'

SELBY'S SECRET DIARY

'Selby! You wrote this, didn't you?' Mrs Trifle demanded, holding out the piece of paper.

Selby stared up at Mrs Trifle, Dr Trifle and Aunt Jetty.

'Now we know that you can talk just like us,' Dr Trifle said. 'And to think, you kept it a secret all this time because you were afraid we'd put you to work around the house.'

'And because you were afraid that if your secret got out you might be dognapped and held for ransom,' Mrs Trifle added. 'Did you really believe that?'

'Were you really afraid of becoming so famous that you'd never get a moment's peace again?' Dr Trifle asked. 'That's what you wrote. It's true that scientists would want to ask you a few questions about what it's like to be a dog, but is that a good reason not to tell us your secret?'

'Okay, Selby,' Mrs Trifle said. 'Now it's time to talk. Come on, say something.'

Selby looked up at his owners, the Trifles, and at Aunt Jetty. He searched for the right words. But what could the right words be?

He thought of saying, 'I beg your pardon, Dr and Mrs Trifle, I'm awfully sorry I didn't talk to you before but ...' No, that didn't sound right. Or maybe, 'Hiya, guys, how are things?' No, that didn't sound right either.

Selby heaved a big sigh.

'How could I have done this to the most wonderful people in the whole world?' he asked himself. 'I've been living a lie. I was so cruel! I've listened to all their conversations, pretending that I didn't understand. I know all their secrets ... and I guess they know *my* secret now.'

Selby's throat went dry. He could feel tears filling his eyes.

'They might have loved me before, but now they're going to hate me. Oh woe woe woe — another horrible, terrible shemozzle! How did I get myself into this?'

As he opened his mouth to speak, Selby's thoughts came flooding back. He remembered that fateful moment only a week before when Mrs Trifle said to Dr Trifle, 'What about a time capsule?'

'What about a what?'

'One of those things you bury in the ground and no one's allowed to open it for a long, long time.'

'But what would we put in it?'

'A portrait of the town,' Mrs Trifle said. 'Not a painted portrait, but something that says what life is like in Bogusville right now. Maybe everyone who wants to can keep a diary for a whole week. Then we'll bury what they've written. A hundred years from now the people of Bogusville — Bogusville will be a city by then — can dig it up and see for themselves just what life was like.'

'Great idea,' Dr Trifle said.

'But what if someone comes along and digs it up a couple of months from now?' Mrs Trifle wondered.

'Don't worry about that,' Dr Trifle said. 'We'll put everything in a steel box and screw the lid on. Then we'll bury it in a ten-tonne block of Quick-Set Super-Hard Killer-Koncrete. Nobody — nobody except someone with a mega-mega-giga-horsepower giant jackhammer — could break into that.'

'Good,' Mrs Trifle said. 'I'll put a notice in the *Bogusville Banner* to tell everyone to start writing about their week.'

★ ★ ★

One week later Postie Paterson delivered a big bag of mail.

'The last of the diaries,' he said. 'Here's mine, too. Have a read of it.'

'Oh, no, I'm not reading them. That would be rude.'

'It's okay. I'll read it to you: "Monday, I delivered the mail. Tuesday, I delivered the mail. Wednesday, I delivered the mail." Do you like it?'

'Yes, very nice.'

'Thursday is more interesting,' Postie said. '"Thursday, I delivered the mail and cleaned the wombat cage at the zoo."'

'Very good,' Mrs Trifle said. 'We want people in the future to know what we did for the week. You delivered the mail.'

'And I cleaned the wombat cage at the zoo,' Postie added. 'Then, on the weekend, I went skydiving but my parachute didn't open and I fell through the roof of a house, which made the house catch fire, but I rescued everyone and ... Sorry, I was just kidding. Actually I read a great book about delivering the mail. I thought I knew everything about it, but I didn't. It was really good. I'd better be going. I've got something to do.'

'Deliver the mail?' Mrs Trifle said.

'You guessed it.'

Later that day the trouble started. And of course it started with Aunt Jetty and Willy and Billy bursting into the Trifles' house when Selby least expected it.

'Hey!' Willy squealed. 'That's that stupid, stinky dog! Let's get him, Billy!'

'You leave Selby alone!' Mrs Trifle said, standing between Selby and the boys.

'But he knows how to talk,' Willy said.

'Yeah, he does,' Billy said. 'Only he's not telling nobody.'

'Now don't be silly,' Mrs Trifle said.

'Here's my diary,' Aunt Jetty said, putting the pages onto the pile.

'What's all them?' Billy asked.

'Lots of people wrote what they did last week,' Mrs Trifle explained. 'We're going to put them in a time capsule so that people a hundred years from now can find out about us.'

'I wanna write somefing too!' Willy said.

'Me too,' Billy said. 'I want to! I want to! It's not fair if I don't get to!'

'All right, boys,' Mrs Trifle sighed. 'There are paper and pencils in the study.'

'And don't you dare write anything rude,' said Aunt Jetty.

'We won't, Mummy,' Willy and Billy said together.

That night when the Trifles were asleep, Selby unscrewed the lid of the time capsule. He tore open the envelope with Willy and Billy's page in it.

'Just as I thought,' he said to himself as he started reading the page.

Sleby is a stink dog. He stinks and he lys cos he sez he kant tawk but he kan tawk lotz and lotz. And his bum looks likke hiz fase and his faze looks lika his bum and...

Selby stopped reading.

'It just sounds unbelievably stupid,' he said, throwing the page into the wastepaper basket. 'No one would believe it. But, hang on a tick, those little monsters have given me an idea. What if I tell my own story in my own words? I can't tell anyone my secret right now, but wouldn't it be great if people in one hundred years' time knew that there actually was a real, live talking dog?'

Selby dashed into the study and started writing. And this is what he wrote:

To the people in the future. My name is Selby and I'm a real dog. My owners are Dr and Mrs Trifle. They are really really great. But they don't know something about me. They don't know that I can talk. And read. And write. If you read the Selby books that Duncan Ball wrote you'll know all about me cos they're really true. I ring him up and tell him my stories and he just writes them down. I couldn't tell anyone about my talking because...

Selby finished writing the page and then put it in an envelope and wrote 'Selby Trifle' 🐾 on it.

'Now I feel so much better,' he thought. 'It's an answer to all my worries. I can keep my secret, but in one hundred years' time the whole world will know everything about me. It's a pity my paw-writing isn't neater. Oh well, that'll show that it was really written by a dog.'

Selby put the envelope in the time capsule and screwed the lid back on.

The next day, Selby, the Trifles and most of the town watched as the capsule was placed in a hole in the Bogusville Memorial Rose Garden. Then a big truck poured in ten tonnes of Quick-Set Super-Hard Killer-Koncrete, which was as solid as stone in minutes.

'I wonder if people in the future will be surprised about what life was like here in the old Bogusville?' Mrs Trifle said.

'I can certainly think of one thing that's going to surprise them,' Selby thought, trying not to snicker.

🐾 *Paw note: Of course I wrote my real name and the Trifles' real name too.* S

Selby tried to imagine what it would be like when the time capsule was opened. Once the people in the future knew there had been a real talking dog in the world, they'd study the Selby books in every tiny detail. People would write more books about him. There would be TV shows — and even movies.

'I will be the most famous dog in the history of the world,' Selby thought.

And that would have been that, except for one little thing. It happened a few days later when Mrs Trifle was putting out the rubbish. As she did, a breeze blew a bit of paper onto the ground. And as she stooped to pick it up she noticed Willy and Billy's writing.

'They wrote what?' Aunt Jetty screamed down the telephone.

'They wrote horrible things about Selby,' Mrs Trifle said. 'I found a draft of what they wrote in the wastepaper basket. What they put in the time capsule is probably a hundred times worse.'

'They will bring shame to my good name!' Aunt Jetty said.

'It's too late now, Sister,' Mrs Trifle sighed.

'What's done is done. It would take a mega-mega-giga-horsepower giant jackhammer to break into that time capsule now. Anyway, I guess it won't matter that people in a hundred years' time think that your boys were badly brought up.'

'We'll see about that!' Aunt Jetty cried. 'Willy! Billy! Come here!'

An hour later Mrs Trifle opened the door, and there stood Aunt Jetty with the time capsule under one arm and a mega-mega-giga-horsepower giant jackhammer under the other.

'I couldn't find the boys' page, but have a look at this!' Aunt Jetty said, handing Mrs Trifle the envelope marked 'Selby Trifle'.

'Why? What is it? "Selby Trifle"?'

'That mutt of yours wrote it,' Aunt Jetty said, pointing to Selby. 'Willy and Billy were right all along. That dog of yours can talk — and read and write. And he's a little sneak, if you ask me. Imagine keeping it a secret all this time and eavesdropping on everyone.'

Dr and Mrs Trifle stood in stunned silence, staring at the page. They turned to Selby and said all the things they said at the beginning of the story. Then Mrs Trifle said, 'Okay, Selby, now it's time to talk. Come on, say something.' (Just as she also did at the start of this story.)

Selby's mouth went dry and tears formed in his eyes and the rest of it, and then, just as he was about to speak, Aunt Jetty burst out laughing.

'What's so funny?' Mrs Trifle asked.

'Don't you see?' Aunt Jetty said. 'Willy and Billy were the ones who really wrote this. See the terrible handwriting? It *has* to be theirs.'

'Do you really think so?' said Mrs Trifle.

'Absolutely! And weren't they grown-up,' Aunt Jetty said. 'They knew they shouldn't write the rude draft you found, so they threw it away and wrote this very clever piece pretending they were that ... that stupid mutt of yours.'

'You could be right,' Dr Trifle said. 'Then the whole thing's a joke. And a good one, too. So I guess you broke the time capsule open for nothing.'

'That's right,' Mrs Trifle said. 'Okay, put the boys' bit of comedy back in the capsule and I'll ring Killer-Koncrete and get another load delivered.'

'Phew!' Selby thought. 'That was a close one! But what a shemozzle! One second more and I'd have spilled the beans. Thank goodness my secret's still a secret. And thank goodness everyone's going to know the truth about me in one hundred years' time after all, because they won't think that Willy and Billy wrote it.'

'Now wait a minute,' Aunt Jetty said, snatching the envelope. 'Let me just write a note on it.'

And with this, Aunt Jetty wrote:

This is just a bit of comedy writing by Jetty's very clever sons, Willy and Billy.

And into the time capsule it went.

'Oh, woe woe woe,' Selby thought. 'I guess my secret will have to stay a secret forever.'

SEE-THROUGH SELBY

'The Kwangdangi Box!' cried Ralpho the Magnificent, the Trifles' old friend and (hopeless) magician. 'It's perfect! It looks just like the real one! It even looks old.'

Dr and Mrs Trifle and Selby had just arrived in the city. Selby followed as the Trifles grabbed the box from the back of their car and carried it into the back of the theatre. There, wearing his magician's cape and tall hat, was Ralpho, ready to do his act.

'I followed those plans you gave me exactly,' Dr Trifle said.

'Yes, I bought those old plans from Luigi Whodunni many years ago.'

'Not the Great Whodunni?' Mrs Trifle said. 'He was the most famous magician ever!'

'This is *sooooooo* exciting!' Selby thought. 'This trick is going to knock the socks off all those other magicians!'

Selby knew all about the Great Whodunni. He'd read a book about him over and over again.

'That guy was the best!' Selby thought. 'He could do any trick there was. He went everywhere and worked out other magicians' tricks and showed people that there was no such thing as *real* magic — it was all just tricks.'

'There's no time to waste,' Ralpho said. 'The MAGIC Show has already started and I'm on next.'

'What exactly is this MAGIC Show?' Mrs Trifle asked.

'M. A. G. I. C.,' Ralpho said, spelling it out. 'It stands for the Mysterious and Ghostly International Conference. This is not an ordinary show. The audience is all magicians. Every year we get together and show off our strangest and spookiest tricks. Wait till they see the Kwangdangi Box trick. It's the most famous magic trick ever.'

As Ralpho talked, Selby remembered the story of the Great Whodunni, travelling on a camel to the town of Kwangdangi in the middle of the desert, where he discovered the Kwangdangi Box trick. There he saw an old magician put a boy in a box, say some magic words — *aka-baka-paka* — and when he opened the box, the boy was gone. Then he said some more magic words and the boy reappeared.

'So this is just like the box that the Great Whodunni saw?' Mrs Trifle asked.

'Not exactly,' Ralpho said. 'It looks the same, but I asked your husband to put a secret hiding place in it.'

'I'll show you how it works,' Dr Trifle said, opening the front of the box. 'The boy steps into the box. It's just big enough for him to stand up. When Ralpho closes the box, the boy lies down and scrunches up as tight as he can. Closing the door brings a flat panel gently down on top of him. Ralpho says his magic words, opens the box, and the boy is gone. Only he's really just hiding in the bottom of the box where you can't see him.'

'And how does he *un*-disappear?' Mrs Trifle asked.

'Simple — Ralpho closes the box again and the panel goes up against the top of the box. The boy stands up, Ralpho opens the box and *ta-da*! there he is. This should really fool the other magicians. They won't have a clue how it's done.'

'So the real Kwangdangi Box didn't have a hiding place in the bottom,' Mrs Trifle said.

'Oh, no,' Ralpho said. 'Luigi Whodunni had a very good look at it. He even took it apart. It was the one trick he could never work out.'

'Maybe it was real magic.'

'Goodness, no! Everyone knows that there's no such thing as real magic,' Ralpho said. 'Ooops! I'm on! Will you two be my assistants?'

'Yes, of course,' Mrs Trifle said. 'But where's the boy?'

'What boy?'

'The one you're going to put in the box and make disappear?'

'Oh, no!' Selby thought. 'He's completely forgotten! Poor Ralpho, he's got to be the most hopeless magician 🐾 in the world!'

🐾 *Paw note: To see how wrong Ralpho's tricks can go, see 'Ralpho's Magic Show' in the book* Selby Screams *and 'Daggers of Death' in* Selby Spacedog.

S

131

'I — I think I forgot,' Ralpho said. 'But maybe one of you can be the boy in the box.'

'Ralpho,' Dr Trifle sighed, 'we're too big. We won't fit. And we certainly can't fit in the hiding place at the bottom.'

'Then where are we going to find a boy — or a girl?' Ralpho said, pacing around the room.

'Let's put our thinking caps on,' Dr Trifle said, pacing around after Ralpho.

'We need someone small,' Mrs Trifle said, pacing around after the others.

'Hey, hang on,' Selby thought. 'How about me? I'm small.'

'Someone very small,' Ralpho said.

'Very, *very* small,' Dr Trifle agreed.

Selby climbed into the open box and sat there waiting to be noticed.

'Yes,' Ralpho said, noticing Selby. 'We need someone about Selby's size.'

'But where,' Dr Trifle said, 'are we going to find someone the size of Selby in the next few minutes?'

'That's right,' Ralpho said. 'Think think think. There must be an answer to this problem.'

'*I* am the answer,' Selby thought. 'Wake up, guys!'

'Look at Selby sitting in the box,' Dr Trifle said. 'Isn't he cute?'

'Cute schmoot,' Selby thought. 'Come on, how about me?'

'Hang on!' Mrs Trifle said. 'How about Selby?'

'Selby?' Ralpho said.

'Selby?' Dr Trifle said.

'Yes, Selby,' Mrs Trifle said. 'It's worth a try.'

Mrs Trifle closed the door to the box. Selby quickly lay down and scrunched up as tightly as he could. Then Mrs Trifle opened the door.

'He's gone!' she cried. 'He did it!'

Mrs Trifle closed the door again and Selby stood up when the board went up.

'And here he is again!' Mrs Trifle said. 'That's the answer! Your disappearing boy is about to be a disappearing dog.'

Ralpho waited with Selby behind the curtain as Dr and Mrs Trifle wheeled the box out onto the stage. Hundreds of magicians suddenly fell silent.

'The Kwangdangi Box!' someone cried. 'The most famous and mysterious trick in the world!'

'But who's the magician?' someone else cried out.

Ralpho pulled the curtain back and bowed. There was a moment of silence followed by a roar of laughter.

'It's Ralpho the Hopeless!' someone yelled.

'Hey, that's not nice,' Selby thought. 'It may be true, but it's not nice to say.'

'Ladies and gentlemen, conjurers and tricksters,' Ralpho said. 'Throw away your trick card decks and your fake handcuffs, because today you will see the most mysterious and ghostly magic ever performed.'

'Yeah, right!' someone yelled, and everyone laughed.

Dr and Mrs Trifle opened the door to the box and turned it round and round on the stage. They stopped when the open door was again facing the audience.

'As you can see,' Ralpho said, tapping the box with his magic wand, 'there is nothing in the box. But before your very eyes you are about to see a real, live dog disappear. Come here, Selby.'

'We'll show them, Ralpho,' Selby thought.

Selby hopped into the box and stood looking out at a sea of tall hats and laughing faces.

'Now you see him …' Ralpho said, closing the door.

Selby quickly lay down and scrunched up as the panel came down and covered him.

'Now does everyone remember the magic words that the Great Whodunni heard when he saw this feat of magic?'

All together the audience called out, '*Aka-baka-paka!*'

Blllllliiiiinnnng!

'That's a strange noise,' thought Selby.

'That's right, *aka-baka-paka!*' Ralpho said, tapping the box again with his wand and then opening the door. 'As you can see the dog is gone.'

'You mean the doggone dog is hiding in the bottom of the box!' someone called out. 'It's the old secret-hiding-place-under-the-floor trick!'

Once again all the magicians screamed with laughter.

'That's cruel,' Selby thought. 'Poor Ralpho. And poor Dr Trifle. He spent all that time making the box and everyone already knows the trick.'

'And now I'm going to bring him back from the beyond,' Ralpho said.

Inside the box, the board lifted and Selby stood up, feeling hugely proud of himself — and Ralpho.

'They may have seen the trick before,' he thought, 'but I'll bet they've never seen it done with a dog.'

The door opened again and Selby leapt out onto the stage, trying not to smile. There was a stunned silence, then more laughter.

'Great training, Ralpho!' someone yelled. 'But you forgot to teach him to come out of the hiding place!'

Dr and Mrs Trifle shot past Selby and peered into the box.

'Selby?' Mrs Trifle said, lifting the panel. 'Where are you?'

'Yes, where are you, Selby?' Dr Trifle asked, tipping the box down to have a closer look.

'I'm over here,' Selby thought. 'Are you both blind or something?'

'Ralpho!' Mrs Trifle cried. 'What have you done with Selby?'

Suddenly there was a burst of applause as magicians dashed onto the stage to look in the box.

'What a trick!' one of them said. 'Congratulations, Ralpho! You had us all fooled. That was the best trick ever!'

'You pretended it was the old secret-hiding-place-under-the-floor trick,' someone else said, 'but you did something else.'

'I take it back, Ralpho!' someone else yelled. 'You are truly magnificent!'

'Ralpho,' Mrs Trifle said, 'could you bring Selby back ... please?'

'I'm right here!' Selby thought. 'Come on, everyone, don't scare me like that. You can see me, can't you? Don't pretend you can't. Hey, I get it. This is a trick on me. But why would they do that?'

Selby looked over at a mirror at the side of the stage.

'That's strange,' he thought. 'I can see everyone there but me. Hang on! Where am I?

Don't tell me my mirror image 🐾 escaped again!'

'How did you do it, Ralpho?' someone asked.

'Well, I … well, I …' Ralpho started as he looked into the box again. 'I'm sorry, but I'm not going to tell.'

'Ralpho,' Mrs Trifle said, 'can we have our dog back, please?'

Selby looked down at his feet.

'My feet have gone,' he thought. 'Someone's taken my feet. Come to think of it, where's my tail, my front paws, my … my … *everything* is gone!'

Selby could see the Trifles on the other side of the crowd being pushed away by magicians trying to get closer to the box.

'Selby! Where are you?' Mrs Trifle called.

By now hundreds of magicians had left their seats and were pulling apart the Kwangdangi Box piece by piece to study it. Selby was kicked and stepped on, being forced off the stage to get out of the way of the crowd.

🐾 *Paw note: See the story 'Selby Splits' in the book* Selby Splits.

S

'Here, Selby!' Dr Trifle called out from the other side of the crowd. 'Come here, boy.'

'I'm over here!' Selby yelled back. 'I'm just invisible, that's all.'

But with the noise of the magicians, no one heard Selby's cries.

It took a long time for Selby to make his way around the crowd to where the Trifles had been, only to see them leaving through the stage door.

'Stop! Wait for me!' Selby yelled, following them onto the street.

Mrs Trifle looked around towards him for one brief moment as she got into the car. By the time Selby reached the spot where the Trifles' car had been parked, it was speeding away.

Selby stood on the footpath for a moment.

'My life is over,' he sniffed. 'I have nothing left to live for. I hope I never see another magician for the rest of my life. I'm sure that no one will ever see me again.'

It was a sad, lonely and invisible dog that walked the streets of the big city, dodging this way and that to keep from being trampled on by a thousand walking feet.

But while this sad chapter in the life of the only talking dog in Australia and, perhaps, the world drew to a close, a new chapter in the life of the only *invisible* talking dog in Australia and, perhaps, the world was about to begin.

Because Selby had a plan . . .

(Which you can read about in the very next story.)

SEE-THROUGH SELBY'S RETURN

(Continued from the previous story.)

Strange things began to happen in the city almost straightaway.

Things that no one could explain.

No one except Selby.

Strange Thing Number 1

In a laneway, two boys were robbing a little girl.

'Give us your money and your mobile phone!' one of the boys demanded.

'But I don't have a mobile,' the girl said.

'Shut up and give us your backpack!'

One of the boys was about to grab the backpack when a little voice said, 'Get away from me or else!'

The boys stopped and looked at each other.

'Did she just threaten us?' one of them asked.

'I think she did. Grab her!'

Suddenly the girl's backpack swung in a big circle, hitting one of the boys on the head.

'Oooooooooh,' he groaned as he fell to the ground.

'Something just bit me!' the other boy screamed, grabbing his leg.

'And I'll bite you again if you don't get out of here,' the voice said.

'Ouch!'

'Ooooh!'

'Ouch!'

The two boys moaned as they hobbled off down the laneway.

The puzzled girl looked around and picked up her backpack.

'They'll never bother you again,' the voice said. 'Are you okay?'

'Yes, I'm okay.' The girl asked, 'Who are you? I can't see you.'

'I'm your guardian angel,' the voice said.

Strange Thing Number 2

A little old blind lady started across the street, waving her white stick in front of her. Suddenly a car sped around a corner, heading straight towards her.

'Look out!' a voice out of nowhere yelled, and suddenly a mysterious force pushed her backwards.

The car sped past, missing her by centimetres.

'Oh thank you, young man,' the woman said, catching her breath.

'You're very welcome,' the voice said. 'Take my hand and I'll help you across the street.'

'You've been most helpful,' the woman said when she reached the other side. 'And, goodness me, you have a very hairy hand.'

Strange Thing Number 3

In a restaurant, a very nervous young man was having dinner with his girlfriend.

'Rachel?'

'Yes, Dudley?'

'Rachel, I want to ask you a question. I want to know if you would … well um …'

'Yes, Dudley?'

'I like you very much and, well, we've been going out for a long time and …'

'Yes, a long long time, Dudley.'

'I like you a lot, Rachel, and I think you like me too.'

'Yes, Dudley, I do. I do. What did you want to ask me?'

'I've been wanting to ask you if you would … if you would be my …'

'Yes, Dudley, what is it?'

'I-I-I don't know if I-I-I can ask.'

'Please, Dudley, ask me. Oh, Dudley, don't be afraid.'

'I, well, I, well, I … wonder if you would … go out with me again next week.'

'Is that all you wanted to ask?! Well, yes, okay,' the girl sighed. 'Now let's eat before the food gets cold.'

Suddenly a voice said, 'Rachel, will you marry me?'

'What was that? Marry you? Oh yes, Dudley, yes, yes, yes, of course I'll marry you! I thought you'd never ask! And you did it without even opening your mouth. How did you do that?'

'I don't know. Somehow it just came out.'

'Well I'm glad it *finally* did. Okay, it'll be a June wedding. I'll wear a white taffeta gown with white silk shoes and my bridesmaids will wear pink, and my brother's rock group will do the music. We'll have a two-week honeymoon on Honeymoon Island and — hmmm, that's strange.'

'What's strange, Rachel?'

'I could have sworn there were ten peanut prawns left on that plate. Now there are only six. Did you eat some?'

'No, it wasn't me.'

Later that day, in the poshest hotel in the city, two clerks were talking.

'How exciting!' one of them said. 'We have a mystery guest in the Grand Royal Super Suite. It's been ages since anyone stayed there.'

'He must be very very rich. Who is he?'

'I don't know. He signed in as a Mr S. Trifle just an hour ago. The first thing he did was call

Room Service and order lots of food. I took the trolley up to his suite and knocked. He called out, "Come in!" When I went in he asked me to leave the trolley next to the spa. The spa was filled with water and churning away but there was no one in it. It was very strange.'

'He was probably hiding in the other room so you wouldn't see him,' the other clerk said.

'I know. I reckon he's a famous movie star and S. Trifle is just a made-up name.' 🐾

Selby sat in the whirlpool spa in the Grand Royal Super Suite of the BigBux Delux Hotel. In one paw he held a slice of Double Raspberry Ripple Cream Cake and in the other a tall glass of Fruit Fandango with a curly straw and a pink paper umbrella.

'This is the life,' he thought as he pushed a button and watched the marble wall open to reveal a wide-screen TV. Selby started to click his way through one hundred and twenty channels and sixty movies.

🐾 Paw note: He was right, of course, because my real name isn't Selby and the Trifles' real name isn't Trifle. S

But his mind was only partly on the spa, the food and the one hundred and twenty channels of TV and sixty movies.

'I love being invisible,' Selby thought.

In the short time he'd been invisible, he'd taken the lift up to the top of the Crystal Tower, 🐾 visited two museums, the aquarium and the zoo, and he'd even taken a cruise around the harbour — and all without paying a cent.

'When you're invisible,' he thought, 'you can do anything you want!'

But the happiest part was helping people. Selby had slipped a wallet back into someone's pocket after they'd dropped it in the street. He'd caught a little boy when he fell off the swings in the park. He'd even knocked the gun out of a bankrobber's hand. He'd done lots and lots of things that made him feel good.

But Selby had a new plan …

'I know I can't stay here forever,' Selby thought. 'But I wouldn't want to anyway. No,

🐾 Paw note: The last time I went up the Crystal Tower I did it the hard way. See the story 'Selby on Glass' in the book Selby Scrambled. S

148

I'm going back to Bogusville and the wonderful Trifles. Only, things are going to be very different.'

Now that he was invisible, Selby would have to talk to the Trifles, of course, or they wouldn't even know he was there and wouldn't feed him or pat him.

They would be shocked at first, but they'd get over it. Then he'd tell them everything about his life. They would have to keep it all a secret, of course, because no one would believe that they had a real, live talking dog, especially if the dog was invisible. Then Selby could go wherever he wanted to and do as he liked. And the best thing of all was ... he would never have to worry about Willy and Billy ever again.

'I was angry at Ralpho for making me invisible,' Selby thought. 'But now I know he's given me a whole new life. I think I'll ring Duncan right now and tell him about what happened.'

Selby had just hung up the phone when a news flash came up on the TV screen.

News Flash!
Magic at MAGIC!
Dog Disappears at Magicians' Show!

'It's being called the greatest magic trick ever,' the newsreader said. 'Today at the Mysterious and Ghostly International Conference magician Ralpho the Magnificent made a real dog actually disappear. The magician is here with us in the studio. How did you do it, Mr Magnificent?'

'A good magician never tells his tricks,' Ralpho said, smiling slightly.

'Yes, but is this dog actually *gone* or is he *invisible*?'

'I don't know. I hadn't thought about that. I think he's gone.'

'Are you going to bring him back?'

'No, I don't know how to. I mean, I don't think I'll do that,' Ralpho said.

'This dog, was he your dog?'

'He belonged to my good friends, the Trifles. They're a bit sad, of course,' Ralpho said. 'I'll buy them a nice new puppy and that should cheer them up. Sorry, gotta go now. I'm getting phone calls from all around the world.'

'A nice new puppy!' Selby said. 'Does he really think he can replace me with any old puppy?'

'Staying with our main story,' the newsreader said, 'we now cross to the home of the most famous magician of our time, the Great Whodunni.'

'I can't believe it!' Selby said, sitting up straight in the spa. 'Whodunni is still alive! I thought he'd been dead for yonks.'

Selby listened as the old magician talked about the Kwangdangi Box, about the boy disappearing, and about how he'd sold the plans for the box to Ralpho.

'I could never work out how the trick was done,' the old man said. 'I guess Ralpho must be a cleverer magician than I ever was.'

'Rubbish!' Selby said. 'You were the greatest! Ralpho was just lucky that Dr Trifle made the box look exactly like the first one.'

Suddenly the faces of Dr and Mrs Trifle filled the TV screen. There were tears rolling down their cheeks as they spoke.

'This is the worst day of our lives,' Mrs Trifle said. 'Our wonderful dog, Selby, is gone forever.'

'I'm not really gone,' Selby said. 'I'm here! And I'll see you tomorrow. Of course, you won't see me.'

'Selby was like our child,' Dr Trifle said.

'Better than a child,' Mrs Trifle added. 'We had none of the problems you get with kids. He didn't complain. He didn't mess up his room.'

'It was just nice seeing him there,' Dr Trifle said, 'lying happily on a newspaper or something. Sometimes we even thought he was reading it.'

'We talked to him just like he was a person,' Mrs Trifle said. 'That's the wonderful thing about pets. They just make you feel good that they're there and you can reach out and pat them. And you can see them and talk to them and they never talk back. And now (*sniff*) we'll never ever see him again.'

'Gulp,' Selby gulped, blinking back a tear. 'This is terrible. They don't want me to be a *talking* dog. They just want to be able to *see* me. They just want me to be the way I always was. Oh, woe woe woe. What am I going to do?'

(Find out in the very next story.)

SEE-THROUGH SELBY'S RETURN (AGAIN)

(Continued again from the previous story.)

It was an exhausted (and invisible) dog that climbed into the window of the old house. The room was dark except for the small lamp on the desk. An old man squinted into the darkness.

'Who's there?' he asked.

'Me,' Selby said, hopping up onto the desk, 'the dog that disappeared at the MAGIC Show today.'

'The what? Is that you, Ralpho?'

'No, it's me, Selby — the dog that disappeared.'

'You're a dog? But dogs can't talk!'

'Well, I can — and I do. But the worst thing now is that Ralpho made me invisible.'

Selby told the Great Whodunni how he learnt to talk and why he kept it a secret. He even told him about the books that have been written about him.

'I read one of those once,' the old man said. 'I kind of liked it, but I never believed it was true.'

'That's because you don't believe in real magic,' Selby said. 'You think that everything is tricks and lies, but it's not. It was magic when I learnt to talk and it was magic again when that stupid Kwangdangi Box made me disappear. When I saw you were still alive, I decided to come here to see if you could change me back.'

'How do you expect me to do that?'

'What were the words that the magician in Kwangdangi said when he made the boy come back?'

'I really can't remember. It was something like *zee moskel*, or *she-munkle*, or *kee-muskle*! Something like that.'

'Oh well,' Selby said. 'It doesn't matter anyway, because you don't have a Kwangdangi Box.'

'Yes, I do.'

'You do?'

'Yes, I brought the original one back from Kwangdangi to study. It's over there in the corner.'

Selby looked over to the corner of the room. In a second he'd leaped down from the desk and was in the box. He pulled the door closed.

'Try to remember those magic words!' he said.

'Well, I don't know. *Zee moskel!, she-munkle!, kee-muskle!*, I just can't remember. It's too long ago.'

'Keep trying!' Selby pleaded. 'Please! My life depends on it!'

'*See-mottle! She-moskle! Ski-momo! Sky-mozzie!* I'm afraid it's just not working. I really can't remember the magic words. I'm sorry.'

'I'm sorry too,' Selby said as a still–invisible tear rolled down his cheek.

'I'll tell you what I'll do,' the old man said. 'Why don't you live here? After all, if I hadn't gone to Kwangdangi this never would have happened. Don't worry, I won't tell anyone about you. It's all my fault, this whole big terrible *shemozzle*.'

Blllllliiiiinnnng!

It was a tired but very visible talking dog that limped back to Bogusville and crept into the Trifles' house to sleep for the night. And it was a surprised and very happy Dr and Mrs Trifle who grabbed him the next morning and hugged him so hard that it hurt.

'Selby, you're back!' Mrs Trifle cried. 'Where have you been? We missed you so much.'

'We certainly did,' Dr Trifle agreed, giving Selby a big hug too. 'We're never going to let Ralpho try any tricks with you again.'

'Oh, Selby, Selby, Selby!' Mrs Trifle cried. 'We love you so much.'

'Yes, we do, we do, we do!' Dr Trifle cried.

'And I love you both too, too, too!' Selby cried in his brain. 'You are the loveliest people on earth.'

'Speaking of Ralpho,' Mrs Trifle said to Dr Trifle after they'd finished hugging Selby, 'I forgot to tell you that he rang yesterday. He wants you to make another Kwangdangi Box.'

'Well, I'm sorry but I just couldn't do it,' Dr Trifle said.

'I agree. Think of how sad people would be when their pets go missing.'

'No, I don't mean that,' Dr Trifle said. 'I couldn't make one even if I wanted to. I found what's left of the plans on the floor of my workroom this morning. They've been destroyed.'

'Destroyed?' Mrs Trifle said.

'Something's ripped them to pieces,' Dr Trifle said. 'They're in little bits with teeth marks all over them. It was almost as if Selby himself had done it.'

Dr and Mrs Trifle both looked at Selby.

'He wouldn't have done something like that, of course,' Mrs Trifle said with a smile, 'but you could hardly blame him if he did.'

And this time Selby didn't want to say anything. He didn't even think anything. He just lay there on his mat trying not to smile at his wonderful owners. He was just a normal talking dog again.

SEE-THROUGH ME

Sometimes I think I'd like to be
The sort of dog you cannot see.
Whenever things were getting dull,
I'd turn myself invisible.

Oh to snap my paw just once a year
And *just like that!* to disappear.
I'd sneak into a pastry shop
And quickly gobble up the lot.

I'd creep up on those dreadful brats
On tippy-toes, just like a cat,

Then breathe in one enormous breath
And *scream!* and scare them half to death.

And when I'm tired of transparency
I'd say goodbye to see-through me
And snap my paw again and be
Just sweet little innocent see-able me.

APPENDIX 1

Selby's Elephant and Mouse Killer Joke

An elephant and a mouse are walking down the street.

The mouse says, 'I hate being small. I'd love to be big like you.'

And the elephant says, 'You could be big like me if you wanted to. Here's what you do. First find the nut of the jub-jub tree and bring it to me.'

'Is that all I have to do?'

'Yes, but the nearest jub-jub tree is a long way away and the nuts are very heavy.'

'No problem,' says the mouse, 'I'll roll it back.'

And the elephant says, 'You'll have to go through lion country.'

'I'll do it,' says the mouse.

'And you'll have to cross a river full of crocodiles.'

'No problem,' the mouse says.

So off the mouse goes.

Two years later the elephant sees the mouse, all battered and bruised, limping back into town. He's rolling a jub-jub nut in front of him. Half of the nut is missing and the rest is covered in dirt and slime.

The elephant says, 'What happened?'

And the mouse says, 'Well, I did what you said. I managed to get through lion country and across the crocodile-filled river and get the nut. But when I was rolling it back through lion country again, the lions caught me and said they were going to eat me.'

'How did you escape?'

'I challenged the biggest, bravest lion. I said, "If I show you that I'm stronger than you, will you let me go?" The lion said, "You? Stronger than me? Ho ho ho. Okay, little mouse, it's a deal." I said, "Let me go and I'll change into my Super Mouse costume." Well, the lion let me go and I rolled the nut into a hollow log. They thought I was changing into my Super Mouse costume, but I rolled it out the other end of the log and into the jungle and I escaped.'

'Very clever,' the elephant said.

'Yes, but then I was caught by crocodiles while I was crossing the river. Again I told them that I was braver than the bravest crocodile. Again I said I had to change into my Super Mouse costume, and again I went into a hollow log and escaped. Anyway, here I am and here's the nut.'

The elephant looked at the mouse. Then he looked at the jub–jub nut. Then, with a twinkle in his eye the elephant said to the mouse, 'I'm sorry but after

---

Department of Health
We regret that we have had to take out the
rest of this appendix in the interests
of public safety.

Now You Don't

How do you feel **now** that you've finished the book? Tired? Exhausted? Well I am. And I'll tell **you** what — after that last adventure I **don't** know if I can go on. I've had enough adventures for a lifetime. From now on I'm going to just sit back with the (wonderful) Trifles and read books (when no one's watching) and just take it easy.

Of course I've said that before. I don't know why but things just keep happening to me.

CYA,
 Selby

ABOUT THE AUTHOR

Duncan Ball is an Australian author and scriptwriter, best known for his popular books for children. Among his best-loved works are the books about Selby, the talking dog. *Selby's Shemozzle* is the thirteenth collection of short stories about 'the only talking dog in Australia and, perhaps, the world'. There is also a selection of stories taken from the other books, called *Selby's Selection*, and two collections of jokes, *Selby's Joke Book* and *Selby's Side-Splitting Joke Book*.

Among Duncan's other books are the Emily Eyefinger series, about the adventures of a girl who was born with an eye on the end of her finger, and the comedy novels *Piggott Place* and *Piggotts in Peril*, about the frustrations of twelve-year-old Bert Piggott, forever struggling to get his family of ratbags and dreamers out of the trouble they constantly get themselves into.

Duncan lives in Sydney with his wife, Jill, and their cat, Jasper. As far as they know, Jasper likes the Selby books. But once when they were thinking of getting a dog, they bought a book about dogs. That night the book mysteriously disappeared. In the morning bits of the well-clawed cover were found floating in the loo.

For more information about Duncan and his books see Selby's site at: http://www.harpercollins.com.au/selby

ACKNOWLEDGMENTS

The author would like to thank Sophie Hamley, Shona Martyn, Lisa Berryman, Allan Stomann, Barbara Pepworth, Tracey Gibson and all the others at HarperCollins Australia for keeping an old dog going (and that goes for Selby too).

SELBY SNAPS!

ISBN 0 207 19731 8

Selby, the only talking dog in Australia and,
perhaps, the world, is back in the
snappiest collection of fur-raising and
fun-filled adventures yet!
So hold on tight as you rocket through
space and time with the perilous pooch
as he deals with a nasty knight and
an even nastier dragon!

And take a deep breath as Aunt Jetty
tears through town on a runaway
toilet leaving a trail of destruction;
then Selby is captured and taken away to
be the ruler of a mysterious jungle tribe;
and if that isn't enough he falls head
over heels in love with the most
gorgeous girl-dog he's ever seen!

But the big question is: will the world learn
that Selby can talk? Only you can
answer that question, so grab this eighth
collection of stories and read it,
and then scream at the top of your lungs:

I know the answer and I'm not telling!

SELBY'S JOKE BOOK

ISBN 0 207 19715 6

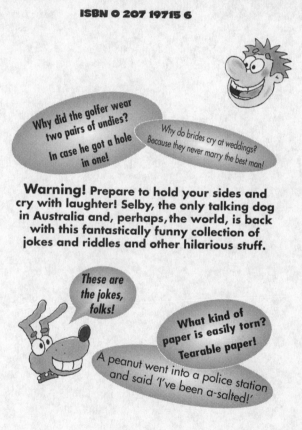

Why did the golfer wear two pairs of undies?

In case he got a hole in one!

Why do brides cry at weddings? Because they never marry the best man!

Warning! Prepare to hold your sides and cry with laughter! Selby, the only talking dog in Australia and, perhaps, the world, is back with this fantastically funny collection of jokes and riddles and other hilarious stuff.

These are the jokes, folks!

What kind of paper is easily torn?

Tearable paper!

A peanut went into a police station and said 'I've been a-salted!'

PIGGOTT PLACE

Duncan Ball

'Tell me what I should do with my life!' Bert wailed. 'Should I catch a boat to South America? Should I learn to play the trombone? Should I start an ostrich farm? I need your help! Give me a sign, any sign!'

Sadly, Bert was talking to the only one he trusted in the whole world: Gazza, his stuffed goat. And, once again, the goat wasn't talking …

Piggott Place is a riotous but touching comedy about twelve-year-old Bert Piggott as he struggles to keep his family of dreamers, ratbags and scoundrels together. Everyone hates the Piggotts and now the council is going to evict them from their once beautiful mansion, Piggott Place. But the authorities haven't bargained on Bert and his young friend Antigone (would-be star of stage and screen) and their crazy scheme. The question is: can two kids take on a world of adults and win?

ISBN 0 207 19979 5